Enjoy these **PRIMROSE U.S.M.C.** titles from
R. Michael Haigwood

First Tour - Rescue
Second Tour - Suitcase
Third Tour - Sleeper Cell
Finders Keepers
Gilt
Squall
In the Name of Justice

Potbelly

R. Michael Haigwood

This is a work of fiction. Names, characters, businesses, places, events, locales, and incidents are either the products of the author's imagination or used in a fictitious manner. Any resemblance to actual persons, living or dead, or actual events is purely coincidental.

Printed in the United States of America

First Printing April 2022

ISBN 978-1-956661-15-6 Paperback

ISBN 978-1-956661-16-3 Hardcover

ISBN 978-1-956661-17-0 eBook

Published by: Book Services
www.BookServices.us

Contents

Potbelly

Thanks to those who gave inspiration for the characters:

Robert J. Nakonieczny, USMC

Michael J. Nakonieczny, USMC

Thomas P. (Mad Dog) Naughton, USMC

H. C. Bowden, USMC

T. J. Martinez, USMC

Two Case Chapman, USMC

Harold Davidson, USN

Gary Kruegar, USN

Ronni Sullivan, Civilian

Gus (Sweet Freddie) Fuson, American Indian

"May God have mercy for my enemies because I won't."
George S. Patton, Jr.

Chapter One

The Cabal

The phone rang relentlessly in the gun store after the mayor of Blaine called a meeting of the town council, demanding that gun ownership and the sale of firearms within city limits be restricted. After the shooting at Virginia Tech, the mayor thought he could save the local high school from any such horror. He didn't stop to think that law-abiding citizens were not the problem. It appeared everyone wanted to spread the blame around, rather than condemn the perpetrator for the carnage. Excuses for the cause of the tragedy were thicker than weeds in a vacant lot.

The murders had been committed by a vengeful student thought to be strange by his peers. No action had been taken against the individual prior to the event, due to rights of privacy. The holy grail of political correctness was paramount at the institution.

In every newspaper, video, and radio broadcast the cause was debated ad nauseam; it was just the blame game over and over: the school, the parents, the economy, society, guns, lifestyle, and America in general. The media was quick to point fingers at everyone except where the blame belonged—on a mentally ill, deranged young man.

There is evil out there in the world, and it paid a visit to Virginia Tech—along with several hundred other places on the same day around the world.

The phone rang again just as the old western-style clock chimed for the dinner hour. Quint sighed. He would answer one more call before closing.

"The gun store, Quint speaking."

The voice at the other end made Quint's heart pick up a couple of beats. The owner of the voice, however, sounded like she couldn't care less about the mayor of Blaine, Washington and his wrong-headed ideas.

"Quint, this is—"

Quint stopped her midsentence. "Hello Sue. How are things in New Mexico?"

Sue let it be known that she was not amused at being cut short. "Quint, a civil tongue would be appreciated! You rogues aren't the cat's meow, you know. I have better things to do than be interrupted by the likes of you and the sort you hang out with."

"Sue, you are a charming woman. I believe dinner, dancing, and cocktails are in order."

There was silence on the other end as Sue, the Cabal's number one negotiator, tried to think of something clever to throw back at Quint, but she could only say, "We need an eyeball-to-eyeball meeting. The board of directors has decided to take serious action in Mexico. It's comparable to the last assignment you and your cohorts were given. If you can manage to find your way here without getting lost, the board would like to see you before the end of the week."

Quint could just see the beautiful, long-legged redhead with the green eyes sitting at her desk and enjoying the banter.

Sue's manner, appearance, and ability to take down the toughest opponent were world class. Her twenty years of field experience made her a valuable asset to the Cabal and the covert operatives that she worked with.

"To make up for cutting me off, you'll fulfill your pledge—cocktails first. There'll be no lame-ass excuses. Don't forget who sends out the checks," she said in a voice that could turn Superman into mush. Or water into ice.

Quint knew when to throw in the towel. He suggested a well-known eatery that had good steaks and lobster and the best wine cellar in the territory. "I'll see you before the end of the week."

The line went dead. Sue had gotten what she wanted as usual, and Quint knew he was in for a special treat from a exceptional woman. Her knowledge of the world wasn't just in the art of death, but also in the art of lovemaking. He smiled as he remembered their last dinner and cocktails, the vision of her still vividly alive.

Sue Battle, a military brat, had traveled the world with her father. Her mother had passed away early in Sue's life, so the military became a constant influence. She became proficient in all the disciplines: hand-to-hand combat, rifles, pistols, logistics, navigation, and, of course, daredevil skydiving—all before graduating from high school.

At the ripe old age of seventeen, Sue enlisted in the army against the wishes of her father, who nonetheless reluctantly signed for her. He'd wanted her to attend one of the military academies, but Sue wanted adventure without delay.

With her superior IQ, officer candidate school and a commission were achieved three years before she would have attained the rank of lieutenant had she attended one of the academies. But the Army career didn't fulfill her ambitions, and after six years of negative responses to her efforts to be included as a regular member of the Special Forces, she decided to resign.

One thing led to another, and she eventually found her place in the world working for the Cabal as a special field agent, roaming the continents and handing out the justice so richly deserved to those who'd slipped through the cracks of civilized society. The Cabal, not a voice for the politically correct game, took action and wasn't squeamish about putting justice before emotion.

Sue's exploits were legendary in the tight-knit, closed society of covert operatives. Skill, cunning, and absolute dedication to the mission were her trademarks. There were those who misjudged her. How could a woman of average height and weight, with a beautiful face and body to match, be a serious threat? Theirs were hard lessons, but they found out soon enough that a captivating smile and manner were not necessarily signs of weakness.

Her green eyes smiling as she replaced the receiver, Sue remembered that last time she and Quint Underwood Michaels had been together. The sparks were real, and they were drawn together like magnets. Their paths had crossed on occasion over the years, but because their skills were similar, they'd never been teamed up for an assignment until a dual-target mission had finally come their way on a hot day in Mexico four years ago. She had a far away look in her eyes as she relived that mission

Sue had picked out the figure of Quint as he disembarked from the ferry that had just arrived in La Paz from Mazatlan. She had always been attracted to him and wanted to know him better, but until then they'd had only cursory meetings.

That had all changed a few weeks before when the Cabal gave them two targets in La Paz—former members of a revolutionary sect from south America, people who had been responsible for the deaths of hundreds of locals. They had become too hot for their bosses, so they were retired to La Paz to live out their lives without punishment for the killings and torture they had committed.

The Cabal had tracked them down and using the latest DNA testing, had confirmed their identities beyond the shadow of a doubt. The two had earned the fate that was about to descend upon them, compliments of the law-abiding citizens of the world.

The killers were an unusual pair. One was a woman of indiscernible gender and the other a male albino. They were both from deep in the Amazon jungle. They had found their way into the outside world purely by accident and been taken in by the leader of a group of revolutionary misfits.

The pair was used solely for killing all those who didn't follow the revolutionary edicts, and they had been busy—to the tune of over a thousand nonbelievers' deaths! Even though the pair's deeds were known around the world, the international community had no stomach for going after them. Being politically correct took precedence over justice.

Before Quint was halfway down the ramp, Sue made eye contact with the six-foot green-eyed man she'd admired for years. This was something more than a meeting of old acquaintances. His brown hair was a little long but neat atop his classically-sculpted face and well-conditioned two-hundred-pound frame. The smile she liked so much was directed at her.

Quint waved as she motioned for him to join her on the dock. When they were within arm's length, Sue said, "Quint, we'll have to go somewhere and put out the fire before we can get anything done!"

Quint gathered Sue into his arms and whispered, "My, my! Whatever do you mean?" There was enough electricity in the air around them to light the local town for a week.

Unlocking from their embrace, Sue pulled Quint towards the end of the dock and a waiting cab. When they were seated, the cabbie took off without a word. Sue had given him instructions before arriving at the docks.

Dodging through the crowded streets, the cab took them to a seedy-looking waterfront hotel in the low-rent district.

Quint was surprised at the location of their digs, but didn't say anything. As it turned out, that was a good thing, for the interior belied the first impression. Inside it could have been mistaken for a hotel in Vegas.

They were led up to their room by the smallest bellhop Quint had ever seen. He couldn't have been much over four feet, although he managed their bags without a misstep. The bellhop took every advantage to explain the room and its amenities.

Quint finally had to grab the short fellow by the collar, slip him a fin, and escort him out of the room. Quint couldn't blame him for trying to enhance his toke. When Quint turned from closing the door, Sue was in his arms. The fire had reached the first stages of a multiple-alarm barnburner.

She was soft in all the right places, and her perfume brought back memories of their few close encounters. Sue's hunger for him was matched by his desire to discover her secrets. Without any pretense of civilized behavior, they attacked one another.

Later, over the noise of the shower, Quint could hear Sue's voice. "The fire is under control, and we'll not be sharing our experience again until the mission is complete."

Damn, what a ball of fire! How could such a wonderful creature turn it off and on so quickly? The ways of a woman are mysterious, to say the least, thought Quint.

"I hear you, Sue. I think you're right on. We can let all the excitement build up again for another time. Business first."

"There they are," said Quint. Through their binoculars, Quint and Sue could see their targets sitting on the hillside near a hiking trail. They were an odd couple: she looked more like a man, and he was a true albino in a land of dark-skinned people.

"This shouldn't be too difficult. We'll follow them to their lair, spend a couple of days observing their patterns, and take our best shot," Sue said as they put their binoculars down.

When the two oddballs started retreating down the hillside, Sue and Quint followed them with their field glasses until they were close enough to see clearly with the naked eye. Once on the side of the road heading for town, they were easy to follow. The pair didn't seem concerned about security, walking about with little attention to their surroundings. Quint remarked, "With their past, these two should be a little paranoid about their environment."

"One thing for sure," Sue added, "they're in good condition. They're walking fast, and the distance doesn't seem to bother them. I don't know about you, but I'm sorta worn out from an earlier encounter!"

The odd couple turned into a small, two-story apartment complex with a courtyard full of colorful local flora in the center. It was pretty much like a garden surrounded by plaster walls and windows. The pair climbed up the stairs to the second floor and entered number three, the apartment directly at the head of the stairs.

Quint and Sue circled the building, discovering ten small garages attached to the rear, one for each apartment. After peering through the window in the door of garage number three, they picked the lock and slipped in, discovering a BMW Roadster and a new Harley Ultra Classic. "Their payment for services rendered must be in the six-figure range," commented Quint.

A further search of the garage revealed bundles of Yankee C-notes stowed in a simple locker against the back wall and in the saddlebags on the Harley.

"Jesus, Sue! There must be half a million dollars sitting in this dumpy garage. They must believe no one would think they were worth more than spit to leave that kind of money lying around."

Sue opened another locker, expecting to find tools, paint, or something of that sort. Instead, she discovered more bundles of cash and a small box full of letters. "Quint, do you read Portuguese? There's a bunch of official-looking letters here written in Portuguese and Spanish."

Quint rummaged through the box and responded, "I can read the Spanish parts. Hang on." He unfolded one of the letters and skimmed through it.

"It appears our two friends haven't retired to live out their lives in seclusion. They're in the employ of some high-ranking officials who want to take out their opposition. That would explain all the cash. I guess leaving it in plain sight may be the best way to keep it safe. Who would suspect those two of being anything but lost souls?"

Quint opened the remaining locker and found a cache of weapons. "Damn, they've got a good variety of firearms here."

Sue responded, "Maybe we should take the cash and spike the weapons?"

"Sue, it might be better to sit on these people for a couple of days and discover their next move. We might be able to eliminate them and lay the blame on someone else. There could be an opportunity to do the world a favor without a ripple in our sails."

"You may be right, Quint, but I'm sure we could make better use of the cash and deny them their weapons too. Let's take the cash, rig up a bomb, and be done with it."

They exited the garage without leaving a trace of their presence.

Walking around to the front and across the street to a small cafe, the two sleuths took seats at an outside table and ordered espresso. From there they could easily see anyone coming or going from the apartment.

"We'll keep an eye on them to see where that leads," said Quint. "If the opportunity comes up, we'll take them out. I'm with you on the cash. When they are out of the picture, we'll confiscate the Yankee dollars, spike the weapons that we don't need, and be on our way. We might as well have the money as anyone else. Maybe donate a major portion to a local church or something. We could put it in the confession booth after hours."

"You're sure in a big hurry to give a million in untraceable cash away, Quint."

"I don't need the money, and I bet the ill-gotten gains of those desperadoes would be better served in the poor neighborhoods of this city than in my account. It's blood money and would surely bring on bad luck. Karma would come into play, and I don't want a black cloud over my head."

"Wow. Guess we better wash our hands of the Yankee dollars as soon as possible! The confession booth sounds good to me," responded Sue without enthusiasm; clearly, she wanted to keep the cash.

At exactly twelve noon on the second day of the stakeout, the oddballs came down and walked around to the garage. Shortly, the sound of the Ultra-Classic could be heard. The bike came around the corner of the alley a little too fast, and the albino had to grab the front brake to keep from crashing into the oncoming traffic. His passenger slammed against his back, her lips in rapid fire as she slapped the albino upside the head.

Quint ran to fetch their vehicle and pulled up to the cafe as the Harley headed down the main drag. Sue jumped in, riding shotgun as they followed the bike. It would be easy to tail them because the loud pipes could be heard, if not seen. There were few Ultra-Classic Harleys in La Paz.

The big bike picked up speed as the traffic began to thin out on the highway leading to Santiago. And lucky for Quint and Sue, there was enough traffic to keep two or three cars between them and the bike.

Quint didn't see any weapons, but then again, they could be armed with pistols under their leather. It was something to take into consideration if action became necessary. It would be easy enough to bump the back of the bike and send them over a cliff into the water, but then they wouldn't find out what they were up to and might miss out on sending some other bad guys to the promised land in the process.

As the outskirts of Santiago came into sight, the bike turned off on a side road leading towards the water. Quint backed off because the traffic had thinned out.

As the road neared the water it began to resemble a serpentine raceway, a challenge for the bike as well as the car. The odd couple disappeared from sight on several occasions, and on the last turn before the beach area, they vanished completely.

Quint continued on down to the beach and brought the car to a stop near a wharf where old fishing boats were tied up to keep them from sinking. There was a small shack at the head of the rickety wooden dock where one could rent a boat or purchase bait, even though there were no boats in sight that could be trusted in water over one's height.

"Where the hell did the bike go?" whispered Sue.

"What the hell are you whispering for?"

"I don't know. It just seemed appropriate."

"Hell, I don't know where the fucking thing went. Some sleuths we are!"

As they exited the car, the Harley roared back up the way they'd come. The odd couple had made them for sure. Quint backed the car around in a power slide and gave chase. It was not a tail any longer, but a pursuit.

With the bike's short head start and reckless speed it was difficult to gain on them, but once they were through the serpentine section of the road Quint caught up to the bike, only to see flashes from a pistol. The dubious female had turned around and was facing them, seated backwards on the rear of the Ultra-Classic.

"Jesus, how did those two live so long? That crazy albino and his bitch should have died back there in the serpentine, and now she's riding backwards trying to hit us with a pistol. Let's back off and catch up with them later. We know where they live," suggested Quint as he let off the gas and they dropped back from the bike, which drew away, flashes still pouring from the pistol.

"What do you have in mind, Quint?" Sue asked.

"I want to backtrack and find the spot where the Harley disappeared. They must have had good reason to turn off there." Quint turned around and headed back towards the beach, slowing at every likely-looking access road.

"Stop, back up," yelled Sue. "I saw some pavement through the brush there. It looks like a likely spot for them to have turned off."

Quint pulled over, but instead of backing up, he parked on the side of the road, hiding the car among some bushes. "Let's leave the car and check out the road. It might be better to search the area with some stealth. No telling what we'll find. Do you have your digital camera?"

They had to fight their way through thick under-brush that led them away from the beach, but in turn shielded them from prying eyes. After two hundred yards of slow going, they pushed through the brush to discover a clearing with a new Lexus sitting in the middle.

They were near enough to see the driver's body slumped over the steering wheel in an awkward manner, while the guy riding shotgun appeared to have a broken neck, the way his head was lying on the dash.

Quint remarked. "I'll go to the left and circle the clearing. You go right, and we'll meet back here. It looks like our friends have taken out some opposition, but we can't be sure they were the shooters. It wasn't long from the time they disappeared on us to when we spotted them again; maybe twenty minutes. Either they're very efficient, or not the perpetrators. Let's be sure before we check out the vehicle any further, since we didn't see anyone but the bikers come out of the bush."

After they made a search of the area around the clearing, the Lexus was next, and it quickly became obvious the bikers had taken out unsuspecting targets. The two in the car hadn't tried to reach for their weapons.

"Sue, take some pictures. Maybe we can find out who these guys are and figure out who the two freaks are working for."

They checked the back seat and trunk for drugs and whatever else might have qualified their occupants for execution.

"Damn! The car is clean as a hospital room. These two stiffs must have been taken out for political reasons," Quint said.

"Lets head back to La Paz," suggested Sue. We'll call in an anonymous tip, and with any luck there'll be something in tomorrow's paper matching names to faces."

"Sue, we were lucky the bitch was a lousy shot. We'd have a hard time explaining bullet holes in the rental. Since they made the car, we best exchange it for a different color and model."

"I like the model, how about just changing the color?"

"It may be academic, since our bikers are probably in Central America by now, and we've screwed up the mission!"

When they returned the car, the rental agent had his ears pointed in their direction while the polite banter continued back and forth between them. The agent handed Quint the keys to their new car, and suggested they stay off dirt roads. He mentioned something about the other car being abused.

"I like the color, but we should have insisted on something more comfortable," Sue said as they headed back to their outdoor table, hoping the assassins were still in La Paz.

"I'll walk around back and check on the garage. You hang out here and keep an eye on the building," said Quint as he walked toward the alley leading to the garage.

Peeking through the dirty window, he could see the Harley was back, but the BMW was missing. The other contents were as they'd left them. As he turned from the window, he heard the sound of an approaching engine. He quickly moved behind a nearby trash bin.

The BMW came roaring in, nearly hitting the door. The albino jumped out, yelling for the bitch to stay put. He hastily unlocked the padlock on the door, pulled it open, and went inside.

Crouched behind the trash bin, Quint had a direct view into the garage. He watched the albino hurry over to the locker with the weapons cache, pick out a shotgun, and rush out, closing and locking the garage door. He jumped back into the car as the bitch was yelling at him the whole time, gesturing with her hands to make her point.

The BMW left so quickly he didn't have time to run around and find Sue. It was getting too dark to follow them anyway. Walking back to the cafe, he thought it would be best to take two-hour shifts, watching the apartments until daylight.

"Did you see the Beemer, Sue?"

"Yes, it squealed around the corner and headed towards downtown."

"Its too dark to follow, how about two-hours shifts watching the apartment? I'll take the first watch if you want to get some shuteye in the car."

"Nice of you to offer, after you traded a comfortable car for that sardine can! See you in a couple?"

Quint, nearing the second hour of his third watch, gave the graveyard-shift waiter a double sawbuck to keep him happy and the coffee coming. At such a late hour the streets were nearly deserted, with only occasional traffic interrupting the quiet. In a couple of hours the sun would make its daily appearance, and the timers on the streetlights would kick in.

Enjoying the silence, Quint was on his third coffee and not having any trouble staying awake, when he observed the BMW roll down the street, pass the cafe, and turn into the alley.

He hurried over to Sue's sardine can, rousted her, gave her a cup of coffee, and told her to get the car running. When she was fully awake, he told her the Beemer had returned, and he was going to walk around back to see what they were up to.

Sue suggested, "Let's do them and get it over with. That's what we came down here for. Who gives a shit who they work for or why? None of our business. Blow the fucking garage up and be done with it."

"Do you want to retrieve the money before we blow the garage?"

"Hell yes."

"Well, then we'll have to tap them first."

"Okay, I'll get the car warmed up and drink my coffee."

"I'll wave at you from the end of the alley if I need you," said Quint.

He gave her a smile and a pat on the shoulder and headed for the alley. Easing up to the window, he peeked in to see them sitting in the car yelling back and forth. It would be a good time to take them out.

Back at the car, as Sue sipped her coffee, a man dressed in a business suit and wearing a fedora tapped on the driver's side window displaying identification and a badge that looked real enough. She pulled her .380 and pointed it directly at the man's chest. "What can I do for you?"

He stepped back and responded, "Where's your partner?"

Before she could respond, the night sky lit up in the alley, followed by a shockwave rocking the car. The suited fedora dropped to the pavement, and the another suit ducked inside the cafe.

She'd not seen the other fellow until he scrambled inside.

Sue leaped out of the car and ran full speed for the alley. As she rounded the corner, she saw the garage ablaze with no roof, the inside charred beyond recognition. The garages on either side were damaged.

With a heavy heart Sue began searching for Quint in the rubble. After a few minutes the two suits showed up, and the one with the fedora asked, "Who the fuck are you guys, and why are you horning in on our project?"

Sue responded, "Who the fuck are you, and what project are you talking about? My partner's missing. He came back here to keep an eye on the odd couple. You've blown him up!"

"I guess our timing's off. The garage went up a little early. But maybe your friend is okay. We'll help you check out the area. We are with the Central Intelligence Agency, and you could have spoiled our play here. Those two scumbags we toasted were part of a plot to kill the U.S. Ambassador. We've been right behind you since your friend arrived the other day. You are meddling in business that is out of your league. You nearly fucked up our hit on the two shitbirds in the Lexus.

Sue's nose wrinkled, and her right brow turned up. "You guys tagged those two?"

"Hell yes. We nailed them right after they met with the bikers. We believe it was a money drop for services rendered."

"Can all the double-talk, pal and help me look for my partner. And did you know you blew up a million in Yankee dollars?"

"Not so fast, lady. What the hell are you talking about?"

"The two dudes had over a million in cash stored in the garage. You two superdicks didn't check inside before you decided to take them out?"

"Our mission here is a success. I suggest you get your asses out of Dodge before the dark side comes down on you."

While they were searching for Quint, he came around the corner of the alley. "What the hell happened here? Jesus, Sue, are you okay?"

"Hell yes, and where the hell have you been? I thought you were under the charred remains of the garage."

"Not so fast, Sue. I've been busy taking care of business. I'll explain when we're alone."

The two suits, seeing Quint alive, beat a hasty retreat. They never said adios, fuck you, or anything remotely friendly.

"Okay, wise guy, what the hell is going on?"

"You have a way with words, young lady. I saw those two plant the bomb, then I followed them back to their car. The fedora walked over to the cafe, and the other one waited for him to start talking with you, then he pulled the trigger.

"The delayed fuse took about three or four minutes. I didn't put a clock on it, but he walked into the cafe when the garage went up. I rifled their car while they were harassing you. It was clean. Who the hell were they?"

Sue explained the situation and then added, "Those idiots didn't search the garage: the cash went up with the roof. We should've taken it while we were there the first time. Damn."

"Relax, Sue, I confiscated half the cash this morning on my second watch. I figured sunrise would be a good time to take them down. The money is in the trunk. Pick a church."

By the time the sun made its appearance, the local authorities were swarming all over the apartment complex. The fire department didn't have much to do, for the explosion had put itself out.

As they sat outside the cafe drinking coffee, Sue suggested, "Let's buy a car and take our time driving up to the border. We can extinguish the fire when it sprouts."

Quint's smile was genuine. "Ten-four."

"Sue, Sue!"

The words brought her out of the fog. *Damn, that episode in Mexico comes in like it was yesterday.*

"Sue, you're wanted on line two. Are you okay? Jesus, you look dazed."

"Not a problem. I'll take the call."

Picking up the receiver, her fingers found line two. "Hello, Sue here."

"Did you find Quint?" the Cabal representative asked.

"Yes sir. He'll be here on Friday."

"Thank you."

Damn that Quint. He's screwed up my whole day. The memories of that rogue made my mind and body tingle all over.

Because of the weather, Quint thought the day would be a bust, but one never knows when opportunity will knock.

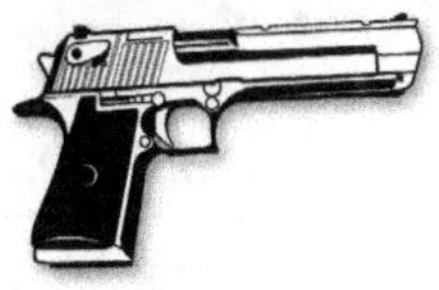

Potbelly

Chapter Two

Homer Kim

"Quintin Underwood Michaels, you may take a seat. The board will see you in thirty minutes," the secretary announced brusquely. She was not a people person, but she could be considered the poster child for efficiency. In the worldwide business of pursuing justice, humor sometimes is left at the door.

Quint was thinking that the time spent cooling his heels at the headquarters of the Cabal could be better spent getting ready for his date with Sue. It had been over four years since their encounter in Mexico. They would soon refresh that encounter with cocktails, dinner, and dancing this very evening.

The flight from Seattle had been uneventful except for arriving twenty minutes late due to a headwind, according to the pilot. A limousine waited at curbside, the driver holding up a sign, *Mr. Underwood.* The Cabal tried to treat all its subcontractors with the respect one would give a colleague.

The limo passed through two guarded gates and pulled into an underground garage. The driver escorted Quint to a special elevator with no markings. He fished a small remote control out of his pocket and pressed a button on it to open the doors. Inside, he pushed number four of the ten listed on the panel.

When the doors opened, the driver said, "Mr. Michaels, the office you're looking for is at the end of the hall to the left. There will be a receptionist there to direct you."

The place looked completely different from his last visit. The previous time he'd taken the elevator up to a meeting room drenched with light from huge windows overlooking the grounds.

Miss Efficiency brought him back to the real world. "Mr. Michaels. The board will see you now. Please follow me." She may not have had people skills, but her figure would qualify for any beauty pageant. It surely made the walk easier, following such a creature. He also kept in mind that anyone working for the Cabal would be armed, well-trained in self-defense, offense minded, and dangerous. Beautiful or not, the receptionist would not be someone to mess with.

"Please wait here." She disappeared through double doors. Moments later, the doors opened and the secretary motioned him inside, where Quint found himself facing a long table, at which sat the board. The attractive woman let herself out.

The boardroom was similar to the last one he'd had the privilege of visiting, but the faces were different, except for his friend Sue, the only female at the table.

No introductions were forthcoming. The man at the head of the table simply said, "Welcome, Mr. Michaels. It's a pleasure to meet you. Your file is most interesting, and because of your record with the company we'd like to offer you an assignment with worldwide implications. It could be the most dangerous mission you've ever attempted. Does it sound interesting so far?"

"Ladies—er...lady— and gentlemen," Quint responded, "I would like more details, of course, but yes, it does interest me."

The men seated at the table were dressed in identical suits. It could have been a board meeting at a huge law firm. Everyone wanted to appear successful, but the lady at the table drew all the light out of the room. It floated around her like the magic powder from Tinker Bell's wand. As Quint's eyes devoured Sue, the suit at the head of the table addressed him. Quint could scarcely hear the suit's words.

"Mr. Michaels, the folder on the table in front of you contains a brief outline of the mission. If you have any questions, please contact Miss Battle."

The words were like a distant echo. Quint picked up the folder and replied, "Thank you, sir. I'll be in touch if there are things here that make my antenna go up." His eyes returned to Sue. He smiled slightly as he anticipated his future conference with her.

"Very well, Mr. Michaels."

The suits rose and filed out, leaving the meeting room like a row of ducklings following their mother, but for one exception, and she couldn't be confused with the ugly duckling. Sue remained seated to answer any questions Quint might have as he thumbed through the folder.

Sue continued, "You know, Quint, as long as we're inside the confines of the Cabal, it's strictly business!"

A beautiful and brilliant woman is intoxicating, especially if she's within arm's length. Concentrating on the folder versus staring at her made for a difficult decision. She noticed the predicament and sashayed over to a door at the end of the room. She pressed a button, waited for the door to swing open, and strode through, leaving Quint alone in the conference room. He finally gained control of his thoughts and put his mind on the papers in front of him.

Quint finished the folder, threw it on the table, and scanned the room. He'd never seen such a dangerous mission in all his fifteen years with the Cabal. It might be an impossible adventure.

He picked up the folder, walked over, and pushed the buzzer for the door that Sue had used. It opened into a private office. Sitting at her desk, Sue smiled and said, "Well, I can see you don't believe what you read?"

"I've been on some ticklish assignments, but this one is out there in fantasy land. It says the details will be forthcoming, I suppose you have them?"

"I do."

"Okay, let's get down to the nitty-gritty." Quint tossed the folder onto the desk. Sue opened the folder and began to read.

"Jesus, Sue, these fuckers are serious about this!"

"Yes, the sooner the better."

"Did you have a hand in planning this?"

"Yes, most of it."

"You are the one referred to as the whore?"

"Yes."

"Who is the third party?"

"Your choice, Quint."

"That's not a hard decision. My partner in the gun shop would be my choice. We've been on several missions together."

"Let's call it a night, Quint. They'll expect you to give them an answer in the morning. I'll expect you to take me to dinner this evening. Pick me up at the front gate at seven."

"How about eight?"

"Seven thirty?"

"Done."

He left the building as quickly as possible. The challenge of leaving nearly equaled that of entering, but he managed to make his way back down to the underground garage, where he found the driver waiting for him.

As the limo departed the gated sanctuary, Quint wondered how an experienced operative like Sue could put herself in such a dangerous situation. The operation she'd had a hand in planning amounted to what some would consider a suicide mission.

He pulled out his cell and punched the number for the gun store.

"Gun shop, Jake speaking. How may I help you?"

In his mind's eye, Quint could see Jake Dahl—thin, six foot two, blond hair, blue eyes—twisting his mustache. He was the best shooter on the planet and a solid partner in the field or gun shop.

"Jake, I need some information pertaining to a mission I've been offered. Would you please find out the best way for three people to illegally enter North Zazakure? And by the way, I volunteered your services to be the third person on the team. You, me, and Sue will be going."

"Thanks, Quint. I don't suppose you thought about asking me first? Maybe I have something else on my plate."

"Never entered my mind. Well?"

"North Zazakure sounds like just the place to spend my vacation. I suppose the timeframe is ASAP?"

"Of course."

"Okay, I'll put out some feelers."

"Cool, I'll get back to you."

The cell went dark.

Quint could see his friend, twisting his mustache again, his eyebrows arched, as he thought about what he might be getting into.

The driver dropped Quint at his motel. Inside the room, Quint called to arrange a rental car and then relaxed and thought about the evening ahead. Sue would be a delight to have dinner with...and maybe more.

When Quint arrived outside the Cabal headquarters at seven thirty, the area was almost deserted; all the daytime employees had left. Sue was standing next to the guard shack. He pulled up to the shack as the guard checked Sue's identification and allowed her to proceed.

She put her head through the open passenger-side window and said, "Hey, big boy! You wanna take a gal to dinner?"

"Sure! Hop in, lady."

"You could be a gentleman and open the door for me."

"I thought you'd never ask."

Quint leaned over and opened the door, and she slid in, leaning close to him.

"Damn! You're a beautiful woman, Sue. I'm speechless."

"Can the shit, Quint. As much as I like to hear those words, I would rather you kissed me and held me."

"If I do that, we might not make our dinner reservations."

"Just do it. I can control our environment."

The embrace lasted longer than either had anticipated and exposed the magic they both felt.

Sue whispered, "Quint let's go eat. I'm getting feelings that require lots of attention, and the car is too small. Let's enjoy a couple of cocktails, dinner, and dancing. I assure you, we can put the fire out in a timely manner."

Quint reluctantly released her; the smell of her perfume and the warmth of her body lingered. She didn't move away, but put her hand on his thigh as they pulled away from the guard shack.

Jake replaced the receiver and dialed the number that information had given him in Vancouver, Canada.

"Homer Kim. May I help you?"

"How the hell did a Zazakuren ever get a handle like Homer? Geez! That's for rednecks in the back country."

"Hello, my friend Jake. Your manners haven't improved."

"Are you free to discuss some important matters?"

"For you and Quint, I have all the time in the world. How may I help you?"

"I just spoke with Quint, and he's accepted a mission in North Zazakure. We need to know how to get two men and a woman across the border without official recognition."

"You know, Jake, not once have you guys ever come up with something simple. This will be a challenge. I'll need to know more details."

"I can set up a meeting with Quint, the woman, and myself. Could you come down to the gun store next week?"

"Sure, no problem."

"I'll give you a call after I talk to Quint again."

"Okay, see you then."

Homer Kim had become a Canadian citizen after his escape from North Zazakure. He'd tried to put a guerrilla army together to overthrow the dictator of that communist country. The south had helped him, but a spy in his core group had dropped a dime on his plans. Most of the members of the group had been executed. Homer escaped with the help of the Cabal. Quint and Jake had been instrumental in bringing him out and saving his family. Kim had been forever grateful.

The waiter had become impatient with the two diners. "Sir, may I suggest a nice red wine to start with while you decide on your order?"

Quint replied, "I believe that would be fine."

Sue said, "Not so fast, guys. I want a white wine."

The waiter replied, "How about one of each!"

"Done," Quint shot back, before Sue could cast a veto.

The wine had been tasted and glasses poured when Quint's cell vibrated.

"What's up, Jake?"

"I called Homer Kim. He's interested in helping us, but wants a face-to-face for more information. I told him we'd meet with him next week. He'll drive down to the shop."

"Damn, you're working fast. Sounds good to me."

"Oh, I almost forgot. He wants to meet with Sue also."

"Not a problem. She can fly into Bellingham and drive up to meet with us."

Sue's expression changed from warm and fuzzy to one of concern. After Quint flipped his cell shut, she asked, "Why the hell would I want to go to Bellingham?"

"Jake and I have a mutual friend, Homer Kim. He's a North Zazakuren by birth, a Canadian citizen by choice. He's associated with a group that has never given up on bringing down the communist regime and uniting his country. Don't be surprised when you are introduced. He is average in height and weight, but has some ugly scars on his face and neck from a shotgun blast in combat. His hair didn't grow back, so he shaves what's left. You'll like him.

"The reason for the visit is to meet with Homer. He's agreed to help us with the mission. With the assistance of his associates in the north, we can get into the country surreptitiously. He wants to meet you and hear in detail your plan. He's coming down from Vancouver to the gun shop in Blaine. You can fly into Bellingham, and I'll drive you up from there."

The waiter returned and inquired, "Have we decided on our entree?"

Quint replied, "Chateaubriand, medium well."

"Wait! I would rather it be just a little pink," protested Sue.

The waiter erased "medium well" and waited for a unanimous decision.

"The lady has the last word," said Quint.

He scribbled on his order pad and with an indignant shrug of his shoulders, proceeded back to the kitchen.

"Do you like the band?" asked Sue.

"Yes. After coffee and cake, maybe we'll be able to dance a little, but I doubt if that would last long. I can feel the heat coming across the table, and I can imagine what a slow dance would bring."

"We could skip the after-dinner drink and dancing."

In the beginning, the touching, kissing, and discovery of each other could have been mistaken for a small riot. Then the passion became soft, slow, and searching. There were little moans as the exploring hands and lips found happy places.

When the fire had been extinguished, Sue remarked, "You know, Quint, I could get hooked on this occasional meeting thing and want more." She rolled out of bed and headed toward the shower.

"I don't think we'd last long. You and I are too independent for the confines of cohabitation. Let's enjoy what time we have together—each time seems like the first."

Leaving the door open, Sue stepped into the shower and turned it on.

"When can you catch a flight?" Quint called.

Sue could be heard over the noise of the shower. "I can't leave for a couple of days. I can meet you up there over the weekend. Throw me a couple of towels."

One towel wrapped around her head and the other barely around her wet body was a picture Quint would like to enjoy more often.

"Okay, I'll take you back out to the Cabal headquarters. How about I give you a warm oil massage before you have to go?"

"I thought you'd never ask."

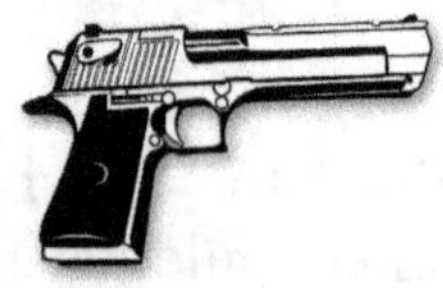

Chapter Three

Blaine, Washington

Jake could see the escape from North Zazakure like it was yesterday. He'd never been so cold in his entire life, and Quint's feet were all but frostbitten. Thinking back on the rescue of Homer Kim, it would have been nicer to give it a go in a warmer month.

Due to the weather, their nighttime high-altitude-low-opening jump had been twenty miles off their target of Soko, a village on the coast. After the HALO jump, trekking through snow up to their knees, with subzero temperatures freezing their faces, made for a miserable night.

Soko's mayor, a boyhood friend of Homer's, had given the two his blessings and sanctuary, putting his own life at risk. But Murphy had stepped all over their plan from the beginning—whatever could go wrong did.

Snatching Homer out of prison was a piece of cake, compared to liberating his wife and three children from an old converted convent that housed the families of political dissidents. The scene of the other women and children, their arms stretched out begging to be taken along, kept coming back.

With the mayor's prestige and a shitload of Yankee dollars they had bribed the prison guards. They were greedy and allowed Homer out for the night. Little did they know he'd be on his way south before daylight, and they'd be taking his cell.

Escorted by two of the guards, the mayor had led them in the direction of the convent. After they had walked for half an hour the mayor gestured to them to stop, the palm of one hand held out, a finger of his other hand pressed against his mustached upper lip. He pointed to the road ahead and the steep incline. The convent perched atop the mountain, silhouetted by the moon on the clear night.

"Jesus!" whispered Jake. "How the hell do they get up there? The fucking road ain't wide enough for anything but a donkey cart."

Kim responded, "There's a tunnel somewhere around here with a shaft leading up to the building. The mayor knows where it is. It is said that the people who dug the tunnel were killed, so no one would know where the entrance was. That was many years ago, and now it's equipped with an elevator, guards, alarms, and video. No one uses the road anymore."

"Kim, you only refer to our friend as the mayor. What's his name? asked Jake.

"That's a long story. It goes back to the Second World War and the Japanese occupation. Moon Jong is his given name, but he's known as Sunny. He thought it better to be in the sunlight than the moonlight. He's an odd character in a family with a history that goes back hundreds of years."

Ahead of them the figure of Sunny towered over the two army guards he had in tow, his thin frame not making much of a shadow in the moonlight.

Kim continued, "There was talk of a wayward Yankee sailor having an affair with one of his ancestors back in the eighteen hundreds, and he inherited the height and round eyes of the sailor. Nevertheless, Sunny is in the fight to unite North Zazakure with its southern neighbor."

Sunny paused and turned towards them. "Gentlemen, these two rats have agreed to help us get into the convent and bring out Homer's family," he explained.

The looks on the guards' faces suggested they'd been scared nearly to death and were willing to do whatever was requested of them.

"Let's be quick about it," suggested Kim. "We have to be at the beach before daylight. The sub will not wait."

Sunny looked at the guards and ordered, "Get going! We'll follow."

In unison, the guards marched off towards the mountain, with Sunny snapping at their heels.

The liberation team halted twenty yards from a shack guarding the shaft elevator. Sunny prodded the two soldiers to step forward and identify their group as official visitors and ask that the elevator doors be opened.

The guards did so, and the doors opened to the largest lift any of them had ever seen. They could all stand with outstretched arms and not touch fingers. The two soldiers looked at each other with wild eyes that didn't go unnoticed by Jake and Quint.

"I believe these two have some bad feelings about the end of this ride," whispered Jake.

"Might be they have some knowledge about what's at the top that they're not sharing with us."

Quint replied, "Kim and Sunny don't appear to be concerned."

Jake pulled Kim into the corner. "These two soldiers are getting more nervous by the second. Do you think we're in for a surprise at the top?"

Kim replied, "Yes, we would have to shoot our way out of the elevator. When the door opens, they'll just spray from wall to wall. But we won't be in here.

"Sunny says there's a secret tunnel beneath the main floor. He can stop the elevator there, and we'll get off, leaving the two guards to receive the bullets meant for us."

"You might have shared that information with us some time ago."

"Jake, we didn't have time for a roundtable conference."

"Okay, but no more in-house secrets. Okay?"

Quint turned from Jake's whispering to Kim in time to see a hand punch a button on the panel, bringing the elevator to a sudden stop. Sunny was smiling at the two guards as he waved for everyone else to exit.

With everyone off except himself and the two guards, he punched the panel again and jumped out as the doors shut. The elevator swooshed upward to the sound of the two left aboard pounding on the door.

Sunny's finger was again on his lips as the sound of gunfire erupted above. The dinner had been served without the main course attending. Sunny's lanky figure headed down the tunnel, long arms gesturing for the entourage to follow.

Turning within a few steps into a short tunnel leading to steep stairs chipped out of solid rock, he bounded up three at a time. Stopping at the top next to an iron door, Sunny motioned everyone to hurry. When they reached the door, he produced a well-used key, inserted it, and opened the door.

As the door swung open, the smell of rice and vegetables rushed out. They were just in time for a late snack. Sunny led the way through the kitchen into a long hallway that ended with more hallways leading left and right. Taking the hallway to the right, he led them to a single door at the end, stopped, keyed the door, and entered, gesturing to everyone to come in. When everyone had entered, he shut the door behind them.

Quint whispered to Jake, "Remember when you were a little kid and you visited China Town, you bought one of those little boxes that it took hours to figure out how to open? Well, here we are in a real, life-size box. The further we go into this mountain, the more the hair stands up on my neck. I don't like being so confined."

"I'm with you, pal. I think we might be in for a shitload of trouble. I don't see any exits."

"Gentlemen." Sunny's hushed voice called for quiet. "Kim's wife and children will be here shortly. They'll come through the door across from the one we just entered. I suggest we lock and load, for they'll be seconds ahead of their guards. On the left you see a naked wall, but it's really a facade. Behind the wall is the entrance to a tunnel that leads down to the ocean.

"When I hear the family running down the hall, I'll pull the facade grating there on the floor, which will release double doors for our escape. On either side of the tunnel are life preservers. Fifty feet from the double doors the tunnel becomes a slide. You'll think you're in Disneyland. It's steep, and at the bottom there's a short turn upward to slow you down before you're pitched into the ocean. A submarine should be waiting."

Kim chambered a round in his pistol and took a position at the door with Jake, who'd already set himself up for the coming battle. Quint and Sunny stood on either side of the camouflaged double doors, their weapons at the ready. When they heard shouting and hurried footsteps coming from the hallway, Kim opened the door.

Sunny followed his lead and opened the double doors.

Kim's family, led by a uniformed soldier, burst through. The soldier never slowed down as they ran through the room and into the open tunnel doors.

Kim and Jake stepped into the doorway, firing down the hall with all they had and catching the pursuing guards unaware. The dead piled up in the narrow hallway, blocking it and slowing pursuit.

While Kim and Jake kept the bad guys at bay, Sunny and Quint helped the family into their life jackets. The soldier leading the escape shed his uniform to reveal a submariner's dungarees. He led the way once again, running down the tunnel and helping the family at the head of the slide.

Kim and Jake emptied their weapons and slammed the door shut. They'd not gotten two feet before the door was full of holes and fell into the room from the concussion of a grenade. They were both slammed to the floor.

Jake made it to his feet, while Sunny ran back out of the tunnel to help Kim. They followed the others through the double doors, as Quint kept up a steady stream of fire at the doorless opening.

The guards were using the dead for shields, throwing more hand grenades into the room. Lucky for Quint, two were duds, and the others hit the wall, bouncing back into the hallway. He knew time was short, but didn't have a clue how to disengage.

Sunny came running back from the slide, grabbed Quint by the shoulders, spun him around, and yelled, "Head for the tunnel."

Quint didn't know what Sunny had in mind, but headed for the tunnel with bullets ricocheting off the walls and ceiling. He felt the warm wetness of blood running down his back and legs, as the shrapnel flying in all directions found soft spots.

Sunny was right on his tail as they entered the tunnel, and when they stopped for life jackets, Sunny pulled another of his invisible levers. Quint yelled, "You have blood pouring from a wound somewhere on your head," as a steel door came down behind them, sealing their escape from the guards.

The limited light had turned to pitch dark as the door hit the deck. In a last ditch attempt to kill them, the guards had thrown a grenade under the door as it cut them off. The sound of it bouncing across the floor gave them an extra burst of energy.

Quint felt Sunny's hands pushing him towards the slide. They were both waiting for the grenade to blow, but it had a slow or malfunctioning fuse. It exploded after they jumped into the slide; their ears and eyes hurt from the concussion in the confined tunnel area.

Quint hit the water first, and Sunny landed behind him. They both recovered from the splash in time to see the sub disappear under the choppy sea.

The sub was leaving at a specific time, with or without passengers. Time had passed more quickly than they'd realized.

Quint yelled over the sound of the choppy water, "What the fuck do we do now?"

"Don't fret, my friend. We have life support, and the beach is only a hundred yards. We'll get to shore, tend to our wounds, and seek assistance from the nearby village."

"Sir, with all due respect, you can't leave my two friends to fend for themselves," Jake said. "There will be hundreds of North Zazakure soldiers after them. We killed a good many of them on the way out, and they're not going to let go. Chances are they were minutes behind us." Jake's face left no doubt about his ire at the captain for taking the sub down before the whole team was aboard.

"I can't put a sub and its crew in jeopardy for the lives of two that may or may not show up. We had a departure time, and that's that," replied the captain. "We would be visible to every shore battery and satellite surveillance system. I couldn't risk that. Sorry, pal."

Homer patted Jake's shoulder. ""Don't fret, Jake. If they got out of the tunnel in one piece, Sunny will figure a way to get ashore at a safe place and then go to the nearest village. The villagers will know him and help."

Jake remarked above the noise of the sub, "Captain, I would venture to suggest that had those two fellows out there been Marines, you wouldn't have disappeared beneath the water. I believe there is some kind of code about leaving wounded or dead on the battlefield?"

"Leave it alone, Jake. I can put you off this boat anytime. This is not a military operation. The rules of engagement are different; very seldom does any mission go as planned. There are always casualties. Who's to say they have been captured or killed? Your friends could just as well be okay as not."

The two wounded warriors were near the beach when spotlights came on and began to sweep the area, the guards from the prison making a frantic attempt to find somebody. There was going to be hell to pay for losing such high profile prisoners.

Even with Sunny's height, the huge rocks gave them cover as their feet touched the sandy beach. Ducking behind the nearest rock, they sat down to take inventory of their wounds, weapons, and ammo.

"The shrapnel didn't embed in my neck, but I can feel some in my legs," Quint said, as he plopped down. "My pistol seems to be okay, but I only have one magazine left."

"Daylight is upon us. Let's move around behind the boulder so they can't see us from the water. The beach is too steep here for them to see us from above."

They scurried around the rock.

"My only weapon is a knife," said Sunny. "I lost my handgun and ammo in the slide. Check my head and see how serious the wound is."

Quint inspected Sunny's wound. "Good news, Sunny; you're going to live. It's a flesh wound, but as you know, head wounds bleed like crazy. What the hell do we do now? It's your back yard."

"The first thing we do is nothing. We'll rest here and give the guards time to wear themselves out. When we're dry and rested, we can find our way up the beach. There is a fishing village not far from here. The cliffs go away, and it's easy access to the village from the beach. I have family there."

"Sunny, how come we're not freezing to death, and there's no snow on the beach here?" Quint asked, as the big guy sat rubbing his arms and legs.

"Chinook."

"You mean the winds?"

Sunny shrugged his shoulders, looked over at Quint, and replied, "No. Warm water and wind. You have them in the Pacific Northwest as well."

"Well, I couldn't be happier about that. The trek from the drop zone was bad enough. I wasn't looking forward to jumping into freezing waters as well. Chinook or no chinook, it's fucking cold. A fire would be nice right now."

"The sun is rising right on time. It will dry us and warm us. The search party will most likely go south, which is good. We'll have an unobstructed way north, where the villagers will hide us and help us get out of the country."

Quint was not sold on the village thing. "How do you know these people can be trusted? Related or not, survival instincts are thicker than blood."

Sunny's frown made it clear he was not pleased that Quint would challenge his family's loyalty. He rose without a word, waved his arm, and pointed north. Off he went, his long legs covering huge chunks of beach with each stride.

Quint jumped up and followed, hoping his new-found friend was right about the village. A Vegas casino wouldn't put out a line on their chances of getting out of Zazakure intact.

"My cousin says he can get us out of here, no problem."

"Jesus, it looks like a problem to me. It's hundreds of miles in any direction to get the hell out of this frozen fucking place. How the hell do you live here year round?"

"Quint, you've led a pampered life. This is a mild winter. And we won't be going by land, but by sea. My cousin says there is a U.S. radar ship in international waters off the coast, and he can get us there."

Quint's shoulders gave a noticeable shrug of relief. "I'm for that. Let's get the hell out of here. And I think we should find the sub captain and do a number on his ass. Maybe Jake already has. When do we head out?"

"We'll have to cool our heels for a couple of days. My cousin usually goes out that way at the end of the week. We'll have to wait until then because his routine has to stay on schedule; anything else would appear suspicious to the coast guard. He says they don't bother this village much, as they supply the army with fish. The soldiers get first choice, and if there is any fish left over, they sell it at the weekly street market to the locals. He wants to send two of his sons with us and claim political asylum. That's a small price to find yourself in safe waters. I'll stay and continue the battle."

"What the hell are you going to do if one of those guards ID's you?"

Sunny, with a broad smile, said, "I couldn't leave here if I wanted to. My family is here, and I want to evict the communists from my land. It's my goal to unite my country once again. I'll hang out with you until my cousin takes you and his sons out to the ship. Then I'll go back home and continue the battle. I'll cross those bridges when they come up."

The radar ship had one ugly profile, but Quint had never seen anything so beautiful. The captain wasn't pleased with all the activity around his supposed covert mission, but he didn't have a choice. The small fishing trawler had nearly collided with the ship in order to stop it.

The captain was really pissed when he heard Quint's story about his escape and the two boys with him.

"This isn't the American embassy, you know. Jesus, you could cause an international incident here, and I'd lose my ship. We nearly ran the fishing boat down, and now you want me to take on refugees. Did you bother to look behind you? There's a North Zazakure coast guard cutter right on your ass. If he comes any closer, we'll have to decide whether to fight or negotiate. That's assuming our navigator has us in international waters."

"Doesn't look like a problem to me, captain," remarked Quint. "The cutter has turned and is heading for shore. The fishing boat is heading north. And there's a sub off your stern. Transfer us to the sub, and your problems are over!"

Jake had heard the story many times, and each time Quint told it, his excitement level rose tenfold.

They would all get to hear the story once again when Kim, Quint, and Sue gathered at the gun store for their strategy meeting.

It would be good to see Kim again, and if things proceeded as planned, Sunny might have an opportunity to see his dream come true.

"You're gonna do what?" exclaimed Quint.

"You heard me. It's the only way to get close enough to the fat puke to kill him," replied Sue.

Kim had arrived early, followed by Sue and Quint. They had a quorum. Everyone involved in the mission was present, and they sat around the workbench throwing ideas around as Sue laid her plans on the table.

"Succinylcholine chloride, *sux* for short. It'll kill him and appear to be a heart problem. Natural death. Piece of cake." Sue was adamant. "I stick him with a needle and voila."

Kim's eyebrows were arched as far as his face would allow as he questioned Sue. "How the hell do you plan on getting into his harem? He's protected like someone in ICU."

"I'm hoping your friend Sunny can help me there."

"He can perform miracles, but getting you inside Potbelly's residence is a major feat."

"I've researched this ad nauseam. He likes round-eyed women from watching so many porno flicks from the West. When I get in there, it'll be easy to entice him."

Quint didn't find the plan tolerable. "What experience do you have as a concubine?" A frown showed through the professional facade.

With the all-knowing look every woman can put forth, she winked at him. "Women have hidden abilities men never take the time to look for. He'll be in a hurry as usual, and all he'll see is a white, round-eyed female. I could be the dumbest blond on the planet, and it wouldn't matter to him. According to his dossier, he tries for three time a day, and I want to be one of those three. He'll be dead before anything serious happens. They'll keep quiet."

"They may decide to kill you to keep the secret."

"Relax, Quint, I'm a big girl, and you guys will be nearby to rescue me. Right?" Sue's expression exuded complete faith in her team members.

"Damn, Sue," retorted Jake. "That's one hell of a bomb to drop on us. You can't expect us to let you enter a harem, pose as one of his whores, and then take him to bed. You're crazy!"

The others nodded in agreement, letting her know they were not in favor of the plan.

"Listen guys, this isn't my first rodeo. I can handle it. It's the best way to rid the world of this tinhorn. We're the only ones who will know it was a hit and not a natural death. All we need is for Sunny to use his connections to get me inside and out. I suppose that's a tall order, but we're not talking chump change here. We can make the world a safer place, and maybe with this dictator out of the picture, the two countries can become one."

Kim's hands squeezed the workbench as he rose. Stretching his arms, he said, "I'll get in touch with Sunny and see what we can work out. I can't promise anything. What you're asking sounds impossible, but then again, Sunny has friends in high places. He says there are those in the inner circle who are not happy with this dickhead and would like to see him disappear. So maybe he can give us what we need."

"If you guys think of a better way to take Potbelly out, I'm all ears," Sue remarked to no one in particular. "It would be nearly impossible to get close enough to tag him with a dart or sniper rifle and get away. We're not on a suicide mission."

"Let's let Kim get in touch with Sunny and explore the possibilities," Quint suggested. In the meantime we'll keep our options open. How about we adjourn for now and meet after dinner to hear what Sunny has to say."

"Don't look at me like that, Quint. You know the ground rules."

Quint was taken aback by the quick comment and responded, "Jesus, Sue, relax. I was just going to ask you out for dinner. No strings."

Sue smiled, "Dinner—and dinner only—sounds good. There's a restaurant a couple of doors down. Meet you there, say, in an hour?"

Quint watched Sue walk to the store's front door. She had a way about her that turned grown men into jelly. He found himself staring, not just admiring. Staring was rude, but he couldn't help himself: he knew what was under those clothes.

"One hour, Sue."

The door slammed without a response.

Kim had been watching the little tug-of-war, and he remarked, "I think you have bitten off more than you can chew, my friend. She'll take you down to zero, and then it'll be up to you to regain your manhood.

The fat potbelly SOB won't have a chance with her. He's as good as dead right now if we can get her into the palace."

Remembering their last encounter, Quint smiled. "She could make me write bad checks."

"There's no hope for you," Kim said as he departed. "I'm going to have Chinese food. You coming, Jake?"

Jake followed him out.

Quint retrieved his pistol, laid it on the workbench, and began to clean it. He had an hour to kill.

The four gathered again at the gun store in the early evening. Quint said, "Now that we've been fed and watered, let's get down to business."

They all looked at Kim, who responded without hesitation. "Sunny couldn't talk because his phone is tapped. He bought a cell on the black market that can't be monitored and he'll give us a call tomorrow. So I guess we might discuss an alternate plan, if Sue's doesn't pan out." Kim looked directly at Sue and added, "I'm not excited about your plan, regardless of how confident you are."

Jake intervened. "Let's drop Sue for now. I have a suggestion." Everyone turned to him in anticipation.

"If the little asshole stands at the balcony watching the May Day parade as he has in the past, we might get a disgruntled soldier to take him out. It wouldn't take much to send an RPG or tank round into the balcony. End of story.

"The shooter might even get away with it. Who knows how many in the military would like to do the same thing, but don't have the balls. There could possibly be a full-scale revolt if the shooter was successful. If Sunny could find just one patriotic soul, it would be an internal thing, and the witch hunters wouldn't be out pointing fingers at the West for the assassination of their leader."

"I'll ask Sunny if such a thing is possible when he calls. That would be an easy solution for us," responded Kim.

Sue's nose and lips were twitching as she listened to the discussion. "That's a suicide mission. Mine is not. Taking him out that way might cause a civil war that could spill over into the south. My way is better. A natural death. Besides, the Cabal has approved it."

Quint held up his hand to silence the chatter. "Let's hold off on anything until we hear from Sunny. He's on the ground and may have ideas we've not considered. A good night's sleep may give us all a new perspective on the situation. How about 0700 at the cafe next door?"

"What'll it be, ladies and gentlemen?" The waitress addressed the table with all the finesse of an over-the-road cattle truck driver.

"Coffee all round, if you please," answered Quint.

She whirled around, dropped the menus on the table, and taking up most of the walking room between the tables and their booth, marched back towards the kitchen. "Damn, we could use her if we run into any trouble," suggested Sue.

After the roller derby prospect delivered their coffee, Quint said, "Let's get down to business. Did you hear from Sunny, Kim?"

Kim set his coffee cup down, rubbed his hands together, and replied, "I have some bad news, some more bad news, and some really bad news. Which do you want first?"

Sue and Jake spoke up at the same time. "The worst first!"

"It goes like this. The really bad news is, the man Sunny had on the inside has been discovered and executed. And the more bad news is, Potbelly will not be on the balcony during the May Day parade. The worst news is that he can't get us into the country or out at present. There is a bright spot, though. He may have another connection inside by the time we're ready. "I filled him in on Sue's plan, but didn't bring up anything else."

Kim's expression changed from uncertain to certain with his last remark. "We have a two-week window of opportunity for whatever we choose to do. That's firm, no wiggle room."

"Let's say we go with Sue's program, and it takes a dump; what then?" asked Jake.

"That's why we're here, Jake. Putting our heads together in case we have to punt," replied Quint.

"Ladies and gentlemen, what we have here is a common problem with unknowns. If Sue's plan peters out, I think we'll be doing all we can to get the hell out of Dodge. I don't think we need to worry about alternate plans. Let's focus on what we have, and if it doesn't work out— Oh well." Kim's remarks didn't fall on deaf ears. Everyone nodded in agreement.

Quint looked around the table for any more suggestions, then said, "As we all agree to focus on Sue's adventure, it's time to put the parts together. Did Sunny mention the cut-off date for us to arrive?"

Kim was slow to answer, taking a great deal of time to be clear about what Sunny had said.

"Yes, our two-week window begins in five days. He suggested we meet in the same village that we departed from a few years ago. The villagers will help us as before. He'll meet us there whenever we decide on a date."

Quint pushed his chair back, stood up, and stretched. "Did he suggest the best way to enter the country, since he can't help us there?"

"He'd intended to help us enter through China, but when his contact inside was executed, that went out the window, so we're on our own in that matter."

"Fang Fat Wing."

Everyone looked at Sue with question marks on their faces. Her voice had a tone that would qualify as presidential as she responded to the looks. "Fang Fat Wing is a dear friend of the family, and he resides in

Taiwan. He is known around the island as Mr. Wing. My father was in China when Wing's small resistance force was decimated by the communists. He helped the survivors find their way to Taiwan, where they are still in the fight against the communists. Although Mr. Wing is ninety, he still has sway over many political figures on the island.

"I believe he'll be more than happy to help take down the fat little puke. I'll get in touch with him today and let you know right away if he can help us get into the country."

Kim smiled as he looked at Sue. "I've heard of Mr. Wing. He's in the import-export business. He'll have connections all over the Far East. Glad to have him on our side."

"Well, are you people going to order breakfast or take up space until the lunch menu comes out?" The roller derby candidate was not being customer friendly on the outside, but her eyes twinkled with humor. "You people stay any longer without ordering, and I'll have to start charging you booth rent. So what will it be? Order something, or begin paying for the space."

Quint handed the menus to her and said, "We'll have crispy bacon and eggs all around, whole wheat toast, and more coffee."

Sue followed, "Throw in an order of biscuits and gravy for us all to share."

"One check?"

"Yes," Jake responded.

She didn't write anything down on the order book as she turned and retreated to the kitchen.

Quint grinned, shrugged his shoulders, and said, "She's like that with everyone. Good gal inside. I've even used her on a couple of simple operations as a bodyguard. She's one tough broad."

Sue stood and excused herself, leaving the restaurant to go use the landline at the gunstore. Mr. Wing was an itch she could only scratch with a one-on-one conversation. Although it would be close to midnight in Taiwan, he could still be at the office. It was a shot. She dialed the last number she'd been given by Wing International.

"Wing International. Stay on the line for English."

Sue waited as the phone clicked. "May I help you?" The voice came across polite and businesslike.

Sue responded, "Please connect me with Mr. Wing."

"Who shall I say is calling?"

"Sue Battle."

The phone crackled as the operator transferred the call to Mr. Wing's office.

"Hello, my old friend." The voice sounded old and frail, but there was a little touch of excitement as he trailed off. "How is your father?"

"He is no longer with us."

"I'm sorry to hear that. He was a good man, and he raised a good daughter."

The words came slow and thick. It was hard for Sue to understand as he continued.

"To what do I owe the pleasure of your company after so many years?"

"Mr. Wing, I know it's been a long time, but I've been very busy working with a group that is trying to set right certain things that official governments are reluctant to address. That's the reason for the call. Can we talk on this line?"

"Yes on my end."

"I'll get right to the point. I need to get myself and three other people into North Zazakure unannounced. I thought you might be able to give us a hand."

"Give me a number to call you."

Sue repeated the number three times before he understood.

"I'll check things out and get back to you. When you say unannounced, do you mean stealthily, or can you go in as a trade mission representative?"

"We need to be there without any public exposure."

"Okay."

The line went dead. The old man had ended the call abruptly.

Sue returned to the restaurant to find the sometime bouncer hadn't left her breakfast on the table, but reordered it when she saw her come through the door. "Your breakfast will be right up." She poured more coffee, gathered all the dirty dishes on the table, and hustled back to the kitchen.

Quint's eyebrows showed concern as he asked, "Well, what did you find out from your friend in Taiwan?"

Sue's hair always looked like she had just left the salon, but today it had the windblown look of a San Francisco Bay Bridge photo shoot. Just the walk back to the restaurant was enough to destroy a hundred buck's worth of salon time.

"Gentlemen, my contact with Mr. Wing went well. He is checking on some things and will give us a call."

The would-be roller derby participant placed Sue's belated breakfast on the table, and while Sue ate, the others chatted about their hair-raising experiences over the years. When she finished, Quint picked up the check, and the four headed to the Gun Store.

Leaving the closed sign on the front door window, they gathered around the workbench. Before anyone could get a word out, the landline began to ring. Jake answered, listened briefly, and said, "One moment please, sir." He handed the phone to Sue.

"Sue here."

You could hear a pin drop as the others sat still when she raised her hand for quiet, as if any movement on their part would interrupt the call. She listened intently, a slight frown on her face.

At the end of the five-minute, one-sided call Sue said, "Thank you, Mr. Wing."

She turned to the others and broke into a smile. "Gentlemen, Mr. Wing has solved our problem of entry into North Zazakure. My friend has a shipment of spare tank parts he bought on the black market; they are headed for the Russian port of Vladivostok. The Russians are sending the parts to Neebo, North Zazakure. Seems Mr. Wing has been the middleman between the Russians and North Zazakure armies. The Russians don't have parts for the used-up tanks they sold to North Zazakure, so Mr. Wing fills the gap and makes a handsome profit.

"We can go in as a technical support team. Once we're in-country, we deliver the parts and the appropriate technical literature. When everyone is happy with the transaction, we head back north, but disappear. He's sending a Zazakuren in with us who has worked for him since the fifties.

"He'll lead us south to Sunyang or wherever our target will be and stay with us until we exit. The country will be in a state of emergency when the little fuck dies, so going back north might be a problem. I think it would be easier to go south, east, or west. Take our leave by the water."

Homer stood up and added his thoughts. "I think there will be different factions standing in the wings ready to take over during the turmoil that is sure to follow. It might be difficult to escape in any direction. I just happen to have the itinerary of the little dictator. I don't want to step on anything Mr. Wing had to say;

he is surely more connected than I am, and things might have changed. But as far as I know, and we can update the information, Potbelly will be attending a meeting in the city of Yampee during the window we have to work with. It might be easier to enter and exit the country the same way. We could go ashore near Yampee rather than travel from the extreme north to the southern border. It would save time, and it wouldn't leave us as exposed as we'd be in such a long journey. Mr. Wing has a fishing fleet, and maybe he could have one of his boats take us near the shore at Yampee."

Sue pondered Kim's suggestion, wondering how far she could push the past loyalty that Mr. Wing and her father had for each other. With the years piling up on him, he might feel his debt had been paid and just say goodbye to her and the past.

"Okay, guys, what do you think? Should we go along with Kim's proposal?"

Everyone looked around, not saying anything. Finally Kim remarked, "Let's remember how far it is from the northern border with China to the border with the south. It would be a long, hair-raising journey."

He turned to a world map hanging on the wall and pointed to China. "I propose we fly into Hong Kong and catch a flight to Tianjin. From there, if Mr. Wing will help us out, we'll use one of his fishing boats to cross the Yellow Sea and go ashore near Yampee."

Homer Kim's eyes were bright with anticipation, his hands shaking. He knew the danger they would all be in from the get-go.

"We can use the same ruse as representatives for Mr. Wing's import-export business. After we take out the lowlife, we'll return to the fishing boat and head for Japan." Kim put the pointer down and seated himself.

Quint searched Sue's face to see her reaction to Kim's suggestion, but she didn't have any expression on her face. She appeared to be in a trance.

"Hello, anybody home?" Jake asked a little too loudly to suit Sue, who shot him an annoyed glance as she snapped out of the fog.

"I'm with Kim on this one. Let's not trek the length of North Zazakure. But there's a problem I see that might kill the whole project. We need to know if Potbelly takes his harem along, and if Kim's friend, or Mr. Wing, can get me on board the road show."

Quint said with little enthusiasm, "Okay, let's go with Kim's suggestion. Sue, put a call in to your friend Mr. Wing. Kim, you call Sunny, and maybe between the two of them we can get some inside help."

Kim stood outside the gun Store and used his cell to call Sunny. As he explained their plan, he could hear chatter in the background. "What's up, Sunny?"

"My cousin is on the extension. He thinks you guys are crazy. He says the coast is locked up tighter than a drum."

"Not to worry, Sunny, we'll come straight into the port of Neebo as part of the fishing boat crew. Right under the noses of the army and coast guard. What we need is transportation from the docks to the little dictator's hotel and back. And, of course, we need to know if he takes his concubines along when he's going to speak outside the palace."

"Yes, he does. It's said he tries for three time a day. How the hell do you plan on getting her into the hotel, let alone into the harem?"

"We haven't worked out all the details yet. Can you get us from the docks to the hotel?"

"Yes."

"Thanks, Sunny, I'll get back to you."

Kim ended the call. He wondered if they might be going down the wrong path. Sue would be in one nasty spot if things went bad. A sniper shot was beginning to look good.

When Kim returned to the gun store, Sue and the gang were sitting around the weapons table in heated debate.

Sue was clearly the loudest. "It'll be just fine, and I say again, this won't be my first rodeo. Jesus, I'm not your little sister, for Christ's sake. This is serious shit, and I'm as serious as you can fucking get!"

Kim interrupted, "Listen! Sunny says he can get us from the beach to the hotel and back. Sue, how did you do with Mr. Wing?"

Sue was still burning at the overprotective numbskulls who didn't appreciate her skill as an overt or covert operations specialist. It was still the "me man, you woman" shit.

"I've explained to these dimwits my considerable skill in getting Mr. Wing to do our bidding. He's offered us a Russian fishing trawler from a small fleet that he operates in the area. We'll be part of the crew. They port in Neebo on occasion, so we won't be out of place. The city is used to seeing round-eyed men and women hanging around the bars and shops while in port. We'll fly into Tsingtao as planned, then to Port Arthur, where a trawler will meet us. We sail across to Neebo. Piece of cake."

Quint had been listening to the banter; now he raised his hand for quiet. "This all sounds good to a point. There is a small problem that no one has addressed: how the hell do we get you hooked up with the short fuck? We can't just walk into the hotel and send you up to his room. We're not in Las Vegas, where the considerable talents of the bell captain would be at our disposal. We need a connection."

Sue stood up again. "You didn't let me finish as usual, Quint. We have all the bases covered. The captain of the Russian trawler has provided the dictator with round-eyed women on occasion. When Potbelly knows the trawler is off the coast, his pimps call the ship for favors. The captain is well compensated for his trouble. Potbelly's team of pimps look for unusual sex partners for his pleasure and will notify the captain to be prepared to send a couple of Russian women to the hotel when the ship ports."

Quint, still not happy about Sue putting herself in such a dangerous situation, asked, "Does the trawler captain send a bodyguard along with the women when they visit Potbelly? We need some way to keep an eye on you in case of trouble."

Sue had the look of a determined sister whose older brother was being overprotective. "Look, Quint, I appreciate your concern. I'm a big girl and a well-trained field agent with years of experience. I can handle the situation. Although if the captain has in the past sent someone along with the girls, I'm all for that. Better safe than sorry."

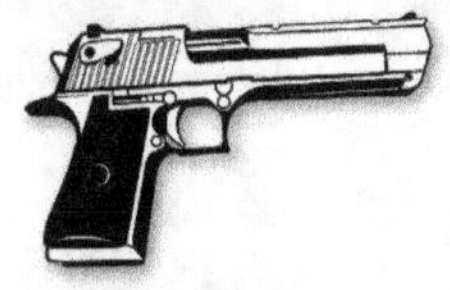

Chapter Four

Port Arthur, China

"Captain, may I introduce the team?"

"Please call me George."

Captain George Bagmanovich was in his sixties, with the wrinkles of command showing the stress of decisions that often meant life or death for those in their charge. He had the look of someone used to getting his way.

He stood at the helm, having to duck under or around most of the overhead equipment. The captain's cover didn't reveal his thinning gray hair, and the brim shaded his blue, twinkling eyes. His smile revealed a sense of humor hidden behind the weathered face.

A former Russian naval officer, he had once plied the North Atlantic, playing tag with British, American, Swedish, and other navies. Retiring from the navy, but not from the sea, he had kept his hand on the helm, the only home he'd ever known. As an orphan he had been taken in by an old sea captain, who passed on to him his love of the sea. He'd never married, but there were women in every port of call waiting for him to return.

Quint, uncomfortable addressing the captain as George, said, "Skipper, may I present Sue Battle, Jake Dahl, and Homer Kim? There are two more involved in this project. They are already in North Zazakure. One is Homer's cousin, and the other an employee of Mr. Wing. We'll meet up with them in Neebo. I don't suppose Mr. Wing went into detail about our mission with you?"

"No. He only requested that I give you all the assistance at my disposal."

Jake took the captain's hand in a firm grip and searched his eyes for any deceit. He found the twinkling blue eyes to be honest and intelligent. *Damn, this guy might be for real. With his help, we may actually succeed in eliminating that potbellied little fuck.*

"Skipper, is there someplace we can have some privacy? Sue and I would like to go into detail with you on our goals."

The captain looked around and suggested, "We could go below to the galley. I'll have the crew stand by topside. Follow me."

Once they were seated, Quint outlined the mission, while Sue filled in the details. The captain sat across from them, his expression never changing, and he didn't interrupt, responding only after the two had finished.

"What we have here is one dangerous mission. If there is any kind of foul-up, chances are whoever is ashore will die." The captain held up his hand as Sue started to rebut him. "But I think we can do this and ship out before anyone knows what happened. I'm willing to give it my all."

Sue smiled. "Thank you, captain."

Quint interjected, "Skipper, have Potbelly's pimps contacted you about your arrival date?"

"Yes, they've been in contact, as many times before. He wants two round-eyed Russian women brought up to the hotel. Sue, you can be one of them. Usually, my number one and I escort the ladies up to the hotel, but this time, Quint, you and I can take care of that. Your people can follow us to help out if things go bad. When the fishing trawlers are in port, no one pays the foreigners any mind."

Sue smiled again, reassured that the two warriors would be close by in case of trouble.

The captain added to his remarks. "The girls are well compensated for their short visits, usually enough to start a new life in a country of their choosing. In the real world you sometimes have to make choices that you're not comfortable with, but reality sets in and you make them based on the rewards. I provide him with girls, they get a chance for a new life, and I keep Mr. Wing's fishing boats from being harassed by the Zazakure navy.

"We'll be doing North Zazakure and the world a favor with him out of the picture. The countries might even step across their border and shake hands once he's gone. The only ones who won't be happy are all the other dictators around the world who support each other.

"One less is good. Since I retired from the navy and traveled around much of the world, I've a better perspective on world affairs, and I agree with the West more than not.

"What about the two people you say are in-country already? We might use them for surveillance prior to our arrival to be sure all is as expected."

Quint answered, "I'll have Kim come below to acquaint you with his cousin Sunny. Sue can fill you in on the man Mr. Wing is sending to help out."

Quint exited through the nearest hatch, returning topside. "Kim, go below. The captain wants to speak with you about Sunny. I think he'll suggest we get him moving on our behalf before we port."

As Kim entered the galley, Sue was telling the captain, "Mr. Wing's man will meet us when we port. I don't know of any way to contact him."

"Okay, let's concentrate on Kim's connection."

The captain turned to Kim and asked, "Can we contact your people today?"

"My cousin who goes by the name of Sunny is hard to reach. He's on the watchlist for the government's spy pool. But I'll be in contact at some point. He'll only answer his cell at certain times and in certain areas. What is it you would like him to do?"

A small frown appeared on the captain's usually smiling face as he answered, "It would be good for him to shadow the hotel where the dictator is staying and keep track of who, what, and where. Surprises are something for amateurs to deal with—we don't need any. When you talk with him, tell him to be vigilant. We need all the information we can get in the event we are pressed to make an unexpected withdrawl.

"I think that'll be all for now. It's late; we'll cast off at eight bells—that's midnight for you landlubbers."

"What do you think, Quint?" asked Jake after the captain left.

"Think about what?"

"The captain."

"Well, if he's as he appears, I'm confident he'll do his best. And since our lives will be more or less in his hands from now on, we don't have much choice."

Jake looked over at Sue and Kim. "Do you have the same opinion?"

They both responded in the affirmative.

"Okay, I agree too."

With the sound of eight bells, they could feel the rumble of the huge diesels as the ship began to pull away from the dock. Over the intercom came the captain's first order. "All hands on deck!"

The crew assembled on the bow of the ship. The captain, standing before the bridge, hands behind his back and leaning forward into the wind, looked like a captain of old. He raised his voice to be heard over the sound of the engines and the wind. "Ladies and gentlemen, this voyage will not be for the purpose of fishing. We are on a special sail this time out. Our employer has made a request of us. We have a job to do in Neebo, Zazakure. It will be our task to deliver our guests there and bring them back. Mr. Wing considers this crew and boat the best in the fleet. We shall prove him right.

"Sophia and Ingrid, report to my cabin. That will be all. Thank you."

The captain, returning to the bridge, motioned for Quint and Sue to follow. He took the helm and asked the bridge watch to go below until he called for them.

When Quint and Sue entered the bridge, Sophia and Ingrid were already standing with the captain.

"Let's get right down to business, people. Introductions are not necessary. The less we know about each other the better. Sophia, you will stay on the ship when we arrive. Sue will be taking your place. You will still receive the compensation you were expecting. You may go below now.

"Ingrid, Sue will join you in the hotel. Your life will be in danger if you reveal to anyone what takes place in the hotel. Since you have been there before, you'll take the lead and explain to Sue what will happen once you're in. You'll be compensated double what would be your usual reward." He looked over at Quint for verification.

Quint considered the prize offered by the captain and said, "Ingrid, whatever you usually get from the pimps for your service, the people I work for will double it. But you have to understand—this will be a life-threatening mission. Would you like to continue?"

Ingrid nodded.

Sue jumped in and explained the details of their pursuit and asked Ingrid if she was still in.

Again Ingrid agreed to be part of the mission.

Captain Bagmanovich spoke with all the authority given a sea captain. "Okay, with that settled, let's get some sleep. We'll be sailing fairly slow across the straits, so we have plenty of time to prepare for the coming events."

Pulling the mike from the overhead, he spoke into the ship's speaker system. "Bridge to crew report, bridge crew report."

Quint asked Ingrid to accompany them below to discuss what would take place when the pimps took them to the short asshole's room.

Chapter Five

Neebo

Crossing the straits was uneventful, even though the seas were turbulent. The captain and his crew were superb sailors.

Shortly after the lights of Neebo appeared in the distance, the trawler's lookouts yelled down to the deck, "Lights approaching on the port and starboard. Coast guard."

The captain had decided to put into port in the dark to avoid any unwanted attention, but it seemed the North Zazakure coast guard didn't appreciate a port of call in the dead of night. Sirens blaring, three cutters surrounded the trawler, yelling through bullhorns to cut engines.

Kim, Sue, Quint, and Jake climbed up to the main deck and stood near the stern as the lead cutter came alongside and the trawler crew threw lines to keep her close.

Kim said, "They're yelling for the captain of the vessel to come on deck and bring his papers. They don't seem very friendly. I thought Mr. Wing had all the bases covered? I think we should start brushing up on our Russian."

Captain Bagmanovich appeared on deck, briefcase in hand. He walked over to the tied-off cutter, and its crew helped him board. The captain disappeared into the bridge as the cutter crew sent four armed sailors aboard the trawler.

Kim suggested they go below to delay any search for passports while the captain was doing his business with the cutter.

What's the hurry, Kim?" asked Sue.

Kim had already hit the hatch to go below, and Sue, Quint, and Jake followed him down. When they were all below, Kim explained, "I thought this mission would be totally covert. If we have to show some identification, I might be in some serious shit. I'll bet they haven't forgotten our escape from their clutches not long ago. I think I should disappear until the cutter crew has left the trawler. I'll hide in the anchor storage."

Just as Kim started to find his way forward, the cutter crew came from the stern and bow passageways. Kim tried to head up the stairwell, but the lead coast guard sailor yelled for him to stand steady.

The sailor and Kim exchanged words for a minute before the other cutter crew members tied his wrist with zip ties. Kim expressed his regrets. "I tried to bluff my way, but as you can see, it didn't go far. They didn't stop the trawler looking for anything or anyone in particular, and since I'm the only oriental on the boat, I drew unwanted attention. They have pictures and long memories, and it hasn't been that long since I escaped the harsh dictatorship. I'll be a prize for their captain to gain some extra privileges."

Kim's voice trailed off as they shoved him up the stairwell.

"Jesus!" remarked Quint. "We have to get the captain on this before they get him on the cutter."

Ingrid popped her head through the hatch and yelled, "The captain is coming aboard. You'd better hurry before they toss the lines."

Quint and Jake bolted up the stairwell and ran down the deck to midships, yelling for the captain. They found him in a loud confrontation with the four cutter crewmen, who had Kim surrounded and were not going to release him.

The captain of the cutter yelled down in English, "Captain, your crew member will be held for further investigation. Please allow my people to return to the ship. Come to the coast guard headquarters while you're in port, so we can bring this argument to a peaceful conclusion. Let's not have a small dispute interfere with our long, uncluttered history of cooperation."

Captain Bogmanovich stepped aside, allowing the cutter crew to board with Kim in tow.

Quint was beside himself. "You're going to allow those thugs to take Kim? What the hell happened to Mr. Wing's protection agreement?"

"Quint, settle down. I just paid them their fee for this month. We can figure out how to get Kim back before we depart. But for now, we don't have much choice. First, we're out-gunned; and second, we don't want to create an international incident and blow your mission. I'll get in touch with Mr. Wing in the morning.

The trawler crew threw the lines to the cutter, and the ships disappeared into the night as the captain set course once again for the lights of Neebo.

"Ingrid," Sue said to the Russian blonde. "Let's go below to the galley. I need to know how things will go once we're in the hotel."

Ingrid led the way, sitting at the first table. "Coffee, Sue?"

"Yes, and let's wait for Quint and Jake to get here, before you share the details of your last visit."

Ingrid Zopodski, a Russian farm girl, wanted to begin a new life in the West. She answered an ad for a cook in the trawler fishing fleet. After a few months at sea, she decided she'd rather be a deckhand than work in the hot galley below. With the deckhand position secured, she studied navigation in her spare time, hoping to improve her value to the ship.

The captain of Ingrid's first trawler recommended her to Captain Bagmanovich, who was searching for a navigator.

When she had a couple of trips with Bagmanovich under her belt, she asked why most of the women on his fishing boat only made one or two trips, and the captain explained the hotel visits with the potbelly asshole.

Ingrid fit the stereotype of a young Russian woman— blonde, with blue eyes and milky white skin—and the captain said she could make enough money in one visit to retire to any place of her choosing. If she made two trips, she would have enough money to retire and take her family to the West.

Quint and Jake arrived and sat down at the table. Sue could see they were still agitated over Kim's capture. She said, "Let's put Kim out to pasture for now and concentrate on the mission. We can deal with him on the way out if we don't have any major problems, or the captain can deal with it while we're busy. Ingrid is going to explain what the procedure is once we're in the hotel."

Ingrid was not used to being the focus of any conversation and was uncomfortable disclosing what she had done and would do again to get her ticket to financial independence and freedom.

"Well, the first thing will be the strip search. The pimps get their jollies doing this. They aren't allowed to touch us, though; they'll just have us disrobe and do a visual search. Then they'll give us the clothing he wants us to wear.

"They won't harm us or put any marks on us. If they damage the merchandise they'll be killed. They leave that up to Potbelly, depending on what kind of party he is interested in at the moment.

"Usually he'll want to see girl-on-girl action first to get excited, then he'll join the party, wanting both girls to service him with oral front and back. He will last a long time, for he will have taken something to extend his performance. We'll be expected to compliment him on his size and stamina, and when he finally wears out, he'll want another show with the girls. This could happen as I say, but he may have moved onto other fetishes I don't know about. I hear he also likes bondage and things of that sort. Don't be surprised if he wants to be tied up and flogged. After the show, he'll trash us for being whores, and tell us we are lucky he doesn't kill us with his bare hands.

"The hard part is leaving. The pimps will try to use us, since he has finished. That's where our escorts come in. You guys will have to stand your ground with these assholes, even if it gets ugly. Otherwise, we'll be subject to any number of rapes and degradation. The money will be wired to Mr. Wing, who will save it and turn it over to us. He has always been fair about that."

Sue asked, "Is there a way to get close enough to stick him with a needle before any of this takes place?"

"No, Sue. He'll not come near us until his little show is over. Then he'll be milk toast and open for your needle."

Sue was having visions of the coming events. She was not looking forward to it.

"Ingrid, I don't know about the show we have to give before we have contact with the target. You'll have to lead the way on that one."

"No problem, Sue, just shut your eyes and follow my lead. It's a one-time thing, and the reward is worth it. For you it's an opportunity to do the world a favor, and for me it means freedom for my family and me in the West. I would have few if any limits to make that happen. If you want, I'll stick him!"

Quint and Jake just sat there listening to the two women. They had nothing to add. It was their show, and it would only work if the two were comfortable with each other. Nothing they could say would make the situation better.

It became very quiet as the four contemplated what Ingrid had revealed about the Potbelly's predilections, but the lull didn't last long, for over the ship's speakers came the voice of Captain Bagmanovich. "All hands on deck fore and aft. Prepare to receive bow and stern lines."

Chapter Six

Detained

The coast guard turned Kim over to the local police, rather than to the army. The coast guard and army didn't get along, each trying to paint a picture of their supposed value to the authorities and unwilling to give the other a reason to shine.

The police interrogator's file on Kim's escape showed pictures of the dead and wounded left behind after the hair-raising getaway through the tunnel to the sea.

With his mug showing up in half the pictures taken from the prison cameras, Kim couldn't deny the accusations. He was just glad that the coast guard hadn't turned him over to the army. That would have been much worse, since most of the dead were soldiers. Their interrogator would have been very harsh, possibly torturing him to find out why he was back in the country and who he was going to meet.

The interrogator kept telling Kim he was going to be executed for killing the soldiers during his escape, but Kim had heard all that talk before. They would be more likely to use him for propaganda purposes.

Kim kept repeating the same answer, over and over. "I never intended to come ashore. I was only on the ship because of the money I would have gotten from an equal share of the catch."

The policeman grew tired of the chase and took his seat behind the desk. He dialed a number and smiled after a short conversation that Kim couldn't quite hear. Then he stood up from the desk and announced, "There is a specialist on the way, who won't be as tolerant. If you don't cooperate with him, he'll call in the army."

The phone jingled again as he walked around the desk towards Kim. He stopped, picked up the receiver, and sat back down. After listening for a few moments, he slammed the phone down, frowned, slapped the desktop in an angry gesture, and rose to his feet. Turning away from Kim, the policeman stalked into the other room and shouted at another officer. "I've been informed there will be a car coming to pick up this traitor. He has enemies in higher places."

Kim didn't like the idea of being taken away from the local police. Somebody with more authority had discovered his past connection with the freedom unification movement, and that would mean bad news for him and for those who had associated with him.

Kim was escorted out of the interrogation office and was sitting near the front window of the police station when he saw a black sedan with diplomatic plates pull up. Two men jumped out. They disappeared from view before they entered the front door. Seconds later the policemen and the newcomers began to argue in two different languages. The two from the sedan were speaking Zazakuren and English.

The policemen were trying hard to be understood as the Canadian embassy people kept repeating their point of diplomatic immunity. They were getting nowhere, so the lead policeman got on the phone to consult his chief. Kim understood both languages and knew the new guys were on his side.

Someone had called the Canadian embassy, and they were here to protect a Canadian citizen. The policemen didn't see it that way and were waiting for advice from their superiors in what had become a delicate international confrontation, way beyond their experience.

As the bickering continued, another car appeared, parking next to the one with diplomatic plates. The lone occupant got out, took a long look at the embassy car, retrieved his cell phone, and made a call before disappearing briefly from Kim's view and then entering. He was dressed in a high-ranking Zazakuren military uniform.

The argument grew louder as the new voice entered the controversy, and just as the situation sounded like it would come to blows, the phone at the front desk interrupted. The policeman answered the phone. "Yes, he's here. General, it's for you."

The uniform took the receiver, "General Fu here."

He didn't say a word, but his face became red, and one could almost see the steam coming out of his ears. Slamming the receiver down, he marched out of the police station without saying a word or even looking back. He got back into his car and drove away. The two policemen looked at each other in confusion.

The phone rang again. The same policeman answered, "Station Two—yes sir." He replaced the receiver and told the Canadian to take the traitor back to their embassy.

Kim thought, *This is too easy. There is something wrong with this picture.*

The policemen cut the zip ties and Kim was led out to the waiting embassy vehicle.

Kim said, "Hey guys, this is too easy. There's something wrong with this whole situation. It might be better if you just let me go, and I'll find my own way. I wouldn't want to be responsible for your injury or death. This looks like a setup to me. How is General Fu connected?"

Everything was moving too fast for the diplomatic corps. The older of the two said, "We've not heard of this General Fu before; he's news to us. And I agree—this picture is out of whack. It might be better for you to take your chances on your own. It's a long ride from here to the embassy, with lots of narrow streets."

"How about you guys dropping me off around the corner?"

"You know, once you're on your own, we'll have to disavow any knowledge of your whereabouts and won't be able to give you further assistance. You will be totally on your own."

"I understand. Thanks for the help. Let me out here. Thanks."

Kim had just exited the black four-door car when it came under intense automatic weapons fire from both sides. He managed to roll into the gutter and slip down an alley out of sight, the thought of the two embassy personnel heavy on his mind as he made his escape. He decided to return to the trawler. That would be the last place they'd look for him, thinking he wouldn't return to the scene of the crime.

Choosing the nearest restaurant, he picked a table in the rear and kept his eyes on the front door as he had dinner. It wouldn't be long before it was dark, and he could find his way to the docks.

"Sue, did you reach Mr. Wing?"

"Yes, his representative will be here shortly. His play to have Kim released didn't work." Before Sue could continue, the trawler's number one appeared on the bridge and announced, "Captain, there is a gentleman to see you."

"Send him up."

The first officer relayed the captain's wishes to the man dressed in a general's uniform, and he found his way up to the bridge.

"Captain. I failed to get Kim released into my custody. The Canadian embassy people were there, and wouldn't deal. I couldn't tell Kim who I was, so

I had to leave without him. Mr. Wing's people called right on time to save my ass. On the way over here I heard that the embassy car was ambushed just after they left the police station. I don't know if Kim was with them or not."

The captain looked perturbed over the lousy start they were having on this important mission. It seemed Murphy had taken up residence on his trawler. "We'll know soon enough. You go below and stow that uniform. Report back up here, we've lots to do."

Using the ship's intercom system, Bagmanovich spoke into the mike. "Sue, Ingrid, Quint, and Jake, would you please report to the bridge?"

When they had all gathered on the bridge, the captain had Mr. Wing's man explain what had taken place so far. The captain added, "Regardless of what's happened, I suggest we keep with the plan and go for the potbellied fucker tomorrow as planned. Ingrid, what do you suggest?"

"I think we have to go with it. He's expecting us, and they'll get suspicious if things don't go as planned. Hopefully Kim wasn't with the embassy car. Who do you think planned the murder of Kim and the Canadians, skipper?"

"I don't think the coast guard just stumbled upon the trawler," answered the captain. "They usually wait until we port to collect their payoff. Stopping us in open water like they did was a dead giveaway. Wanting to collect their bribe money was only an excuse to take Kim and hold him for trial, and when that failed, they ambushed the embassy car. Whoever wants him dead didn't think it through or see that they'd end up with a huge international incident made public all over the world by morning.

"There is one good thing coming out of this: we might be able to do our thing under the radar of tomorrow's headlines. We'll know before long if Kim was in the embassy car or not; until then we can concentrate on our exercise for tomorrow."

Quint spoke up. "If Kim was compromised, we must have a leak somewhere. Tomorrow's mission may also be on the chopping block. Where do we start to look?"

The captain looked over the assembled group and shrugged. "I'll start at the source with a call to Mr. Wing as soon as we find out the status of Homer Kim. I'll go through the crew records, paying particular attention to the newer members, but I don't think it's from this end."

Sue asked, "How many of the crew have cell phones? That might be a place to start if there are any doubts about a crew member."

"Speaking of cell phones, Kim had a cell," remarked Jake. "You'd think if he wasn't in the ambush, he would have given us a call."

"We'll know about Kim soon enough. Let's adjourn for this evening and meet at 0500 for breakfast," replied Captain Bagmanovich.

Leaving the captain on the bridge, the others went below to the galley and had another round of coffee while they discussed once again their roles for the coming events. Sue was speaking when Quint's cell vibrated on the mess table, moving around like a jumping bean. Quint snatched up the tiny phone and looked at the screen. He didn't recognize the call number. Everyone at the table watched nervously as he flipped the lid and said, "Quint here." His face took on a serious look, then a big smile, then concern again. "You're where? Jesus, Kim, stay out of sight. We'll be up to help you."

Quint closed the cell and said excitedly, "That was Kim! He's hiding in the warehouses on the dock. He wants to know if there are any police or soldiers watching the trawler. We'd better go topside, bring the captain in on the turn of events, and try to come up with some kind of diversion to distract the spying eyes of the dictator's secret police."

Kim was hiding in a square of warehouses almost directly across from the trawler mooring. The only light visible came from a number of ships that had their own power generation. There was a light mist falling, making the worn-out pavement slick. The call to Quint had been a last resort, made with a phone he had taken from a patron in the restaurant. It was a miracle that it had worked.

"There was little movement in the dark warehouse area, and he couldn't be sure where the prying eyes were. Getting back to the trawler would be his only real chance to get out of Zazakure alive. His past here had sealed his fate if caught again. He was fortunate the coast guard had taken him, and the events that unfolded after his capture hadn't been his last.

It was impossible for Quint to call him back, for he'd tossed the cell a few blocks away in case it was under some kind of nationwide monitoring, as with Sunny's cell. He would have to keep a sharp eye and ear out for any thing unusual that would cover his run for the trawler.

Keeping his breathing and heart rate at a reasonable level became more challenging the longer he stood in the dark mist wondering if this was his last night on earth. So many things were running through his mind, it was hard to stay alert for an opportunity to make good his escape.

As he was trying to calm down, a patrol of soldiers appeared through the mist and passed not two feet from his hiding place behind an oversized packing box. Luckily for Kim, they were near the end of their watch and not very alert.

They had marched beyond him not more than twenty feet when the sky lit up as bright as a sunrise. The whole dock area was shaking as if a major earthquake had just struck. The shock wave from the explosion knocked Kim and the passing soldiers to the ground just in time, as debris was flying in all directions. Had they not been decked, the flying objects could have cut them in half. Kim jumped up quickly and lit out for the trawler, but to his chagrin the trawler had broken away from its mooring. A small tsunami following the shock wave had ripped the lines loose.

Aboard the craft deckhands could be seen throwing life rafts to anyone who'd been tossed overboard. Not knowing what else to do, Kim jumped into the water as close to the trawler as he dared, hoping that a life raft or vest would find him. He would be just one of the crew being rescued in the confusion.

Fortunately for Kim, Jake, who'd been thrown overboard, saw him jump and swam to help, a compact, two-man life raft in tow. "Well, it looks like you found a way to get aboard unnoticed!"

"I can assure you, Jake, I didn't have anything to do with that blast. I'm just happy as shit that the trawler isn't damaged and you guys are all right. Jesus, what was it that went up?"

"I don't know. I was talking to Quint and Sue, and the next thing I know I'm in the water watching you jump from the dock. We'd better look around for the rest of the team; God knows where they might be."

The captain was on the bridge yelling with a bull-horn. "I suggested a small diversion, Quint. I didn't want you to blow up the whole fucking harbor. Jesus, what were you thinking?"

Quint and Sue were lying on the stern of the trawler deck in a heap of equipment. Both were stunned and couldn't figure out what the hell the captain was yelling about. The ringing in their ears made them nearly deaf. The captain looked like someone doing a mime show on stage.

Jake and Kim scrambled into the small life raft and paddled toward the ship, hoping to find their friends aboard, for they hadn't run into anyone in the water. It was pitch black except for the fires on the dock and some of the ships casting eerie shadows all around them, making it easy to overlook someone swimming nearby.

As Jake and Kim were helped aboard, emergency vessels of every description were arriving in the area looking for survivors and putting out the many fires on the docks and ships.

Quint and Sue were trying to untangle themselves from the equipment the floundering ship had piled on them. They had been thrown together as the shock wave and small tsunami rocked the trawler from stem to stern. As they lay on the aft deck in a virtual knot, Sue whispered so quietly that Quint almost didn't hear her, "Damn, the fire just rekindled. If we were any closer, we'd be connected. Whatever it is you do to me, it's in full force right now."

Before Quint could make sense of what she was saying, the ship rolled and they were thrown from port to starboard.

He thought, *How the hell can she be thinking about a fire burning between us at a time like this, when any normal woman would be verging on panic?*

When they were finally able to stand, Sue saw Jake and Kim being helped aboard. She punched Quint. "Look, Kim's found his way back. I wonder if he had anything to do with the explosion?"

The captain was still on the bridge with his bull-horn. "All hands to your stations. Secure the deck and prepare to throw lines fore and aft. Special passengers report to the bridge."

Jake and Kim stepped over the debris scattered across the stern of the boat to help Sue and Quint finish getting untangled from the ropes wrapped around them from head to toe. Jake was laughing out loud at the sight of the two bound up like a couple of hog-tied calves.

Kim pointed to the bridge. "The captain is not in a good mood. I might better have stayed ashore."

With the ropes cleared, they headed for the bridge. When the four entered the bridge's port hatch, the captain was in his chair looking out at the confusion on his boat. He looked every bit like an old canvas sailing master, ready to hang a crewman from the yardarm.

Captain Bagmanovich turned to face the port hatch as they entered. His face was stone cold, and his eyes bored holes in the special guests. "Well, who the fuck blew up the docks? Which one of you had the balls to destroy everything within a half mile, in every direction from my ship?

"Kim, nice to see you. Somebody came very close to destroying this trawler, which I might add is your only ticket out of this hellhole."

Kim responded, "I didn't set off the explosion although it provided a nice diversion to make my return."

"Okay, if not you, then who? Quint, did you over-play your hand, maybe fuck up and ignite a munitions dump on the docks, or something similar?"

"No, sir. I don't have a clue what the hell happened. We're in the dark, same as you."

The look on the captain's face didn't reveal if he believed anyone or not. His manner didn't change as he looked over at Kim and said, "You, Kim. Get on the phone and call the friend you refer to as Sunny. I want to know what the hell went down here."

Kim responded, "I'll call him at first light."

The captain looked out the forward windows with disgust at the thought of completing the mission in the morning; their prospects were slim to none. The damn port and town would be on alert and clamped down, the army running all over like ants on molasses.

He wanted to complete his assignment and get the hell out of this unpredictable nation. There was nothing worse than being stuck in a country run by a sadistic, spasmodic, lunatic tyrant.

Quint had Kim put on a decent disguise and along with Mr. Wing's man, they took a tour of the docks and warehouse areas as daylight began to expose the devastation. It was a total disaster. Some of the more fortunate ships were still afloat, but there was no dock to tie up to. They stumbled upon the epicenter of the explosion accidently, but turned away, not wanting to be stopped and questioned.

Kim said, "I heard one of the investigators say a munitions ship was off-loading its cargo when it just exploded, creating a chain reaction. As you can see there was a mix of ships with different cargos, with little attention paid to their volatility. In a smartly run port there wouldn't be a mix of munitions and fuel oil docking alongside each other."

As they headed back to the trawler, Kim's cell vibrated. "Kim here."

"Hello, Kim, this is Alice. I'm Mr. Wing's private secretary. He's out of the country on a business trip, but he wanted me to get in touch with you about your friend Sunny. I have some bad news and some good news.

"The bad news is that Sunny was killed in a fire-fight after the explosion last night at the docks." Her voice was business-like, not revealing any emotion—if she felt any.

"Sunny and his patriots had just given their cause a jump-start by destroying the port facilities used by the dictator to import and export his drugs and international black-market goods. The money from these drugs and goods goes into his personal account to keep up his extravagant lifestyle, while the average citizen lives in poverty. They put up one hell of a fight, but in the end were outnumbered and outgunned. Their stand will be remembered in song and poem. The explosion and gun battle have drawn more people out of their shells to fight the communist dictator and his henchmen.

"The good news is that Potbelly will still be in the hotel as planned. He won't allow anything to interrupt his fetishes.

"Mr. Wing sends his condolences and suggests you take advantage of the confusion and complete your task. When you're finished with the man he sent to help you, take him out of the country with you. He wants to try a hand in the West.

"Mr. Wing also said Potbelly was paranoid about what has happened and will send his car for the girls, rather than have them find their own way to the hotel. He was usually paranoid the other way, not wanting anyone to see his car near the docks and round-eyed women from a Russian trawler entering the official limo."

The cell went dark. Alice had disappeared into the international world of global communication.

Kim explained the long conversation with Alice to Quint and Mr. Wing's man, who was pleased to hear he might get a chance at leaving the country and heading to the West.

Quint remarked, "Okay, let's get back to the trawler and get the show on the road. We have about two hours before the limo shows up."

The three returned to the trawler, where they found Jake, Sue, and Ingrid in the galley. Captain Bagmanovich soon came down and met with the team at the mess table.

"Ladies and gentlemen, shortly it will be time to put our adventure into play. According to Kim, our target will send a car for the girls, and we'll not have to worry about escorting them through town with the security out there on edge and trigger-happy. I'll have the trawler warmed up and ready to sail when you return. Good luck, and Godspeed." The captain saluted the assembly and returned to the bridge.

When the captain had departed, Quint asked, "Do we have a vehicle to tail the limo?"

Mr. Wing's man reported, "We have two vehicles ready to chase the limo. It won't be hard to follow; we know where it's going."

Jake interjected, "If we run into any checkpoints, they'll wave the limo through and check us. I think we should have one car follow the limo and the other leave earlier and go directly to the hotel and be there when the limo arrives, just to be on the safe side."

There was a unanimous agreement to split the cars, so Quint moved on. "Jake, you and Kim follow the limo. I'll head over to the hotel with Mr. Wing's man and stake out the front and rear entrance. Sue, you and Ingrid will probably be out of our sight at times, which is something I don't like, but it can't be helped."

Sue remarked, "We'll both be armed. If it goes bad before we get to the hotel, I'm sure we can take out a couple of pimps."

"Okay then, let's go topside and get things moving. The limo will be here shortly."

A minute later they stood on the deck looking at the dock and warehouse area; it was a total debacle. Between the devastation and the hundreds of soldiers, gridlock was an understatement. There were hundreds of military and civilians milling around without a clue what to do. If there was any leadership, it wasn't obvious. The police were chasing looters, and the army was tied up trying to guard what was left of the docked ships and warehouses.

Jake and Kim followed Mr. Wing's man down the gangway into the confusion on the docks. He pointed to a nearby warehouse that hadn't been damaged from the explosion and led them over to it. The warehouse was empty except for two Mini Coopers sitting in the middle of the cavernous building. He pointed to the red one for Jake and the blue one for himself and Quint.

Jake protested, "Why do you and Quint get the blue one? I like blue better than red. Every policeman on the street will see red before blue."

Mr. Wing's man threw Jake the keys to the blue Cooper.

Kim suggested, "Let's pull around to the side of the building and wait for the limo there. We'll be out of sight and ready to take up the tail." They jumped into the blue Mini and positioned themselves to be ready when the limo arrived.

Mr. Wing's man returned to the dock as Sue, Ingrid, and Quint were coming down the gangway. He told them that Jake and Kim were ready for the limo and that their vehicle was standing by. They could jump in and head for the hotel anytime.

Quint still had doubts about the mission and the danger Sue and Ingrid would be in when they were out of arm's reach. Putting his hands on Sue's shoulders and looking deep into her eyes, he said, "If for any reason you're not comfortable with the situation, you opt out. Kim and Jake will be right on your tail to the hotel, and I'll be there when you arrive. If you decide things are not going well and want out, we'll follow your lead. See you there."

"Not to worry, Quint, I'm a big girl, and Ingrid knows the ropes." Mr. Wing's man waved at Quint and pointed at his watch. Quint squeezed Sue's hand and remarked, "You be damned careful."

Mr. Wing's man quickly led Quint to the warehouse and the red Mini. Quint was riding shotgun as the Cooper headed for the hotel through a haze of blue smoke, passing the limo coming in the opposite direction. The show was finally on the road.

Kim and Jake were sitting in the blue Cooper when Potbelly's limo pulled up to the dock where the girls were waiting. There was a driver and a guy riding shotgun.

When they stopped, the guy riding shotgun got out and held the door for Sue and Ingrid. He was a huge fucker, his proportions those of a sumo wrestler. The driver never let the steering wheel out of his hands. The sumo type had telltale bulges that revealed he was packing heat.

The limo drove off slowly, dodging all the confusion on the docks, the army guys waving the limo through the mess.

Jake followed as close as he dared to take advantage of the crowd moving aside for the limo. It would be a slow journey to the hotel, which was okay with them.

Inside the limo, Ingrid looked over at Sue and remarked, "We're not going in the right direction for the hotel. They made a wrong turn back at the end of the last block. We better see what's going on."

Sue, crawled up to the open privacy window and put her .380 in the driver's ear. She asked, "Have you made a wrong turn, pal?"

He put up one hand and claimed, "No speak English."

At about that time, Ingrid had the guy riding shotgun around the neck with her knife pointed at his throat. She spoke his language. "I would appreciate a good answer."

Shotgun mumbled something and Ingrid slit his throat. The blood began to gush all over the front of the limo, and the driver looked over just in time to see his partner slump into the dash, dead to the world. He locked the doors on the limo and tried to run the privacy glass up, but with little success: Ingrid had blocked the glass with her purse. She yelled for him to pull over.

When he eased over to the curb, Sue asked who had hired him. Ingrid repeated the question. There was a lot of gibberish that was hard to figure out, but finally Ingrid said, "He says a man from Taiwan gave them a nice chunk of money to pick us up, take us to the local dump, and kill us. But he was only going to drop us and then disappear, keeping the money."

While Ingrid was telling his story to Sue, the driver reached down to an ankle holster and tried to surprise them. Sue shot him in the ear twice, one round coming out through the window and the other through the door. She leaned over the front seat and unlocked the doors. Then she got out of the back seat and opened the driver's side, shoving the driver's dead body into the middle of the seat so she could jump behind the wheel.

"Ingrid, where the hell do we go?"

"Hell, I don't know."

Just then Sue's cell vibrated for her attention. "Sue, it's Captain Bagmanovich. Another limo just showed up for your ride to the hotel. Something is rotten in Denmark. Get the hell out of the limo at your first opportunity!"

"We know, Captain. We've just killed the two drivers and are now looking for a place to dump the bodies."

Sue was still on the cell when Kim and Jake ran up to the limo. They'd parked a discreet distance away and were puzzled to see Sue getting out of the limo and jumping into the driver's seat. Ingrid gave them a quick recap of the situation and asked, "What the hell do we do now?"

Jake retorted, "Leave the fuckers here. We'll use the Cooper and put some distance between us and the stiffs."

They all ran back to the Cooper, piled in, and headed for the hotel.

Quint's cell vibrated in his shirt pocket as he and Mr. Wing's man found their way through the bicycle and scooter traffic of the busy port city. "Quint here."

The voice of Captain Bagmanovich came through loud and clear. "Hang on to your hat, Quint, and don't show any signs of surprise. The guy with you is not Mr. Wing's man. The asshole with you killed him. He's an imposter. Wing just found out about the betrayal and advised us. Do what you think is best, pal. The limo that showed up was not the one from Potbelly. I warned Sue and Ingrid of the situation, but they'd already figured it out and killed the two kidnappers.

"They are headed for the hotel with Kim and Jake in the Cooper. I told the real limo driver that the girls were taken to the hotel by my crew members because of the confusion. They bought it and are on their way back to the hotel. Good luck, my friend."

Quint closed the cell and said to the impostor, "That was the captain. He says everything is going as planned. He's one long-winded dude! How far are we from the hotel?"

Quint hoped the sweat on his forehead wouldn't seem out of place to the impostor. That damned Murphy had surely taken up residence on the ship and was now following the team around making a nuisance of himself.

Quint was thinking, *I'd better wait till we get to the block where the hotel is located before I take him down. Jesus, what the hell will I do with the body? Think, man! I wonder what the others did with the limo stiffs?*

The impostor motioned to Quint and pointed up the street. There was a hotel sign less than a block away. Half the block in front of the hotel was roped off, with guards checking vehicles. None were being allowed any farther up the street.

The impostor turned right at the corner and drove around to the alley behind the hotel. He smiled at Quint and parked the car about halfway to the rear exit.

Quint gestured for the impostor to stay put and got out of the Cooper. He slowly walked around the rear of the car and approached the driver's door.

The driver sensed something was up. He locked the door and tried to start the car, but Quint already had his knife out. He smashed the window with the hilt of his knife, clipping the man on the forehead with just enough power to delay his starting the car. Then he quickly flipped his wrist and plunged the knife blade into the man's left ear all the way to the hilt. He died without a sound.

Quint rolled the broken window down and pushed the dead man's head onto the steering wheel like he was passed out. He put the car in neutral and let it roll down the alley until it hit a light pole. It would look like a drunk driver had passed out. He then walked around to the street in front of the hotel to wait for the team to arrive.

Jake said, "Damn. Look! Half the block is roped off, and they're checking every vehicle. We'd better pull over and figure out how the hell to pull this off."

When Kim pulled over to the curb, he almost ran over Quint, who was frantically waving his arms at them. Kim yelled out, "Jesus, there's Quint. I almost ran him over. He must have discovered the impostor. I wonder what he did with him."

Jake replied, "What bothers me is who hired these guys and what was their plan?"

Quint opened the door and said, "The real limo is behind you. We need to wave them down and transfer the girls. We'll never get past the guards." The questions they all had would have to wait until the mission was accomplished.

Quint added, "Kim, you get out, and when the limo comes up the street, wave it down, and the girls will jump in. I'll go to the other end of the block and walk down as close as I can get to the hotel entrance; you guys do the same from this end. Be ready to take out some guards and rush in if need be.

"Sue, if you and Ingrid smell a rat, don't hesitate to bring the house down. If that means grabbing someone's gun and shooting Potbelly, instead of sticking him, so be it. There'll be so much confusion, we might actually get away. It wouldn't hurt my feelings if you had to shoot your way out rather than lie down with that pig."

"Time will tell. Here comes the limo," Kim said excitedly. He waved down the black four-door Mercedes.

The limo pulled over. Kim opened the rear door, leaned in, explained that their car had broken down; they couldn't deliver the girls to the hotel. The driver was happy to find the girls, not wanting the dictator to punish them for not doing their job. He'd executed others for less.

Kim loaded the girls into the limo, and the driver pulled away thanking his stars he would be showing up at the hotel with undamaged goods.

Quint watched as the Mercedes was waved through the roped-off area by the soldiers manning the checkpoint. Then he crossed the street and walked up to the corner to take his position at the end of the block, kitty corner from the hotel.

Jake and Kim stayed with the Cooper, hoping they'd be able to get Sue and Ingrid back to the trawler in one piece. Their view of the front entrance was unobstructed. The limo stopped, and the guy riding shotgun leaped out and opened the rear door.

Ingrid was first out, leading the way into the hotel lobby. Sue was right on her tail. The two escorts hurried to catch up to them.

The two white-skinned, round-eyed women drew a lot of attention, but onlookers kept their heads down and avoided staring. No one wanted to have a problem with the two evil-looking escorts.

It was obvious where the women were going and whom they would see. The dictator's reputation had preceded him.

Chapter Seven

Ingrid Zopodski

Sitting in the back of the limousine, Ingrid's past flashed through her mind in vivid color—the highs and lows of her childhood and her years as a young adult trying to escape to the West. Her thoughts rushed at her in a dizzying vortex as the Mercedes pulled into the circular drive in front of the hotel.

"Ingrid, pay attention! Do you want to grow up with an empty head?"

The teacher was of the old mold, dressed like the women from the farm country. Her stern manner was reflected in the fear in every child's eyes—except in Ingrid's. At the age of sixteen, Ingrid thought about everything in the world but school, considering it a waste of time. She wanted to get out and see how other people lived, not just those in the Soviet Union. Her spare time in the past few years had been spent reading worldly books from her grandfather's collection, kept hidden in the basement of their small home. The books were not allowed, for they were not written by, or approved by, the tyrannical government.

She dreamed of taking the train to the West, to see London, Paris, Rome and—the wildest of all dreams— the United States of America, the land where people were free to move about, read anything they wanted, vote for their government, own a business, and attend a church of their choosing.

The only thing holding up her dreams was the thought of leaving behind her family and fear of what might happen to them if the government wanted to punish her through them. But those thoughts passed as she saw herself on a plane to America.

Ingrid began planning her adventure at the ripe old age of ten. The only persons who shared her dream were her grandmother and her childhood friend Axle. She had met Axle in the first grade and knew from the beginning he'd be her husband someday. They'd shared some of the books, and their dreams inter- twined. They were of the same mind when it came to leaving the old country and trying for the West.

The teacher waved her pointer in Ingrid's direction and swatted the big desk at the front of the class. "Ingrid! You will leave this class and not return until you can focus on the lessons provided for your benefit by the great Soviet government's loving and caring education commissar." Ingrid bowed to the old hag and slammed the door on her way out, never to return. She would find some day labor to help her grandmother and study on her own. They wouldn't bother her if she was doing manual work for the good of the people's republic. The workers gave their all to Mother Russia.

Axle had long ago separated himself from the choiceless society and had gone underground to undermine the government that chained its people to the unproductive, repressive, godless Soviet Union and its two-class order. There were the ten percent who worked for or were in the government. They lived well off the backs of the ninety percent who were all equally poor, which was the dream of their socialist masters.

Axle and Ingrid dreamed of the West, where the roles were reversed, where ninety percent of the population were equally well off and ten percent were under the radar, with an opportunity to join the others with practiced skills and hard work. The couple just wanted the opportunity to fulfill their dreams of freedom, but getting to the West would prove to be difficult.

Finally the day came. Ingrid stood by the old boat looking over the seawall. Axle was running down the beach, chased by his Malamute. Her heart skipped a few beats every time she saw Axle. The feelings had been in her from the first grade. He waved as he saw her and changed directions, making the dog stumble and run into his legs. They both fell to the sand and rolled, the dog getting to his feet first and running toward Ingrid. Axle jumped up, smiling, and chased the dog towards her. As always, his smile captivated her. His shining blue-green eyes and his dark wavy hair blowing in the wind always induced a warm and fuzzy feeling in her stomach.

When he reached the seawall, she climbed over and fell into his arms. They were strong and wrapped around her with the might of a giant, but the gentleness of a lamb. He was tall and a little on the thin side because he'd been running from the government most of his teen and adult years.

"It's all set," he said as he hugged her, pressing her to him, knowing she would be his for all time. "We board the fishing vessel tonight. Our quest has become reality. The West is in sight."

Ingrid squeezed the only lover she'd ever known or wanted. He made her feel like the whole world was theirs for the taking. If there was a private moment on the vessel during the night, he would make love to her as never before; she could feel the vibrations coming from him. The excitement of their new adventure would make the loving wild and passionate. Keeping it under control would be a problem in the cramped quarters of the ship.

Now they made love on the deserted beach, slowly, with the caressing more meaningful than ever before. Axle whispered things in her ear that made her tingle from head to toe. This time it was slow, the searching exciting. The next time, on the boat, would be erotic and crazy with the thoughts of freedom letting their souls reach out as the chains of repression were released.

That was the last time she held Axle.

The secret police had found his hideout and followed him to the beach. They were sadistic fuckers, letting them think their lovemaking would continue to the new world.

When the police pulled him from her, he resisted a little too much, and the shots rang out. He slumped over Ingrid and with his last breath said, "I love you; I love you. Don't give up."

They dragged his body off the beach and put Ingrid in the police vehicle for a ride to the station, where she was tortured beyond belief because she wouldn't break down and reveal the names of other resisters.

Her scars were not visible to the untrained eye, but her body had been used in any manner of ways to please her interrogators.

And then one day, out of the blue, the cell door opened. The guards disappeared. All the inmates just wandered around, not knowing if it was a setup to shoot them all for trying to escape. Finally, a voice came over the loudspeakers. "Everyone report to the exercise yard."

Once they were all gathered in the yard, the speakers blared again. "The prison is now closed. You are all free to find your way to wherever you please. The Soviet Union is no longer. You are now in Russia. If you are arrested for any reason from this day forward you will be placed in a suitable institution for your crimes."

After years of hard work and a lot of luck, Ingrid had found the fishing fleet of Captain Bagmanovich. Her ticket to the West had finally been punched. Her memory of Axle's last words had motivated her through the rough spots. Going into this hotel now might be the last day of her journey. The risk and whatever they had to do to finish the mission paled compared to what had beset her before. She shook her head, trying to get the past out of her mind and put the operation on the front burner.

"Sue, stay as close to me as possible," Ingrid had whispered as they walked up to the entrance doors. "They'll take us to a special room, and we'll be strip-searched. Where did you put the syringe?"

"I put it between the cheeks of my bum."

The pimp led the way to a small room for the strip search, and you could tell he enjoyed this part of his job, taking his time eyeing them after they had removed their clothes. He didn't touch, just glared at them, envious of his employer.

When he was satisfied they didn't have anything to harm Potbelly, he handed them each a robe and led them to another room a few doors down. Once in the next room, four young ladies took them into a large bathing area, took their robes and washed them from head to toe. Perfume was applied and they were given sheer kimono-like gowns.

The lead bather said, "You will wait here for further instructions."

As they waited, Ingrid remarked, "It's going just as before. It won't be long now."

After all the dressing, undressing, and bathing, Sue finally had a chance to remove the syringe and put it in a more comfortable hiding place under her arm. "Ingrid, what will he expect from us after the show?"

"Well, it's hard to say. I've talked to the other girls on occasion, and they all had different stories. But there are a couple of things we all had in common.

"He'll want oral sex with one of us after the show. I'll let him do me, and while he's busy, you stick him."

"What if he's not alone?"

"He's always been alone, from what I understand. He doesn't want to share his perversion with anyone. Whether he has someone in the wings watching, I don't know. In any event, it will be an opportunity to take him out. He likes a lot of light in the room while he's doing his thing. I think he may be going blind."

They hadn't waited long before there was a light knock on the door, and one of the regular paramours peeked. "Please follow me," she said.

Ingrid took the lead, wanting to be the one Potbelly saw first and maybe get him to go with her right away and not do the girl-on-girl thing, so Sue could stick him, and they could get out of this hellhole.

As the paramour led them to a room a couple of doors down the hall, Ingrid remarked nervously, "I don't like what's going on here. This hasn't been his routine in the past. We might look for an opportunity to abort the mission and disappear into the crowded streets."

Sue looked around and figured the window was as good a way as any to make their way out of the building. Since they were armed with only a syringe, their options were limited.

She checked the window. It was nailed shut. "I think we'll have to take our chances going out the door and down the hall. I'll check the door."

Sue walked over to the door and pulled on the handle. It was locked.

"Ingrid, you get behind the door, and I'll stand to the side. When whoever comes through we'll take our best shot."

They didn't have long to wait. Within five minutes there was a knock on the door, which Sue hadn't expected. She said, "Come in."

There was the sound of a key, and then the door slowly creaked open. The bath lady who had brought them to the room stuck her head in and ordered, "Follow me."

Sue motioned for Ingrid to lead the way.

They were taken to another room farther down the hall. The bath lady opened the door and waved them in. The carpeted room was equipped with a huge bed in the middle, with lights and cameras strategically placed for a voyeur to enjoy the action. Two chairs took up one corner of the room. Sue and Ingrid, not knowing what else to do, seated themselves in the chairs.

Another paramour entered the room from a door near the head of the bed. She instructed them, "The blonde woman will place herself in the middle of the bed. The redhead will stay in her seat."

Ingrid nodded and rose, whispering to Sue, "Maybe this will work out after all." She moved from the chair to the middle of the huge bed. The paramour followed her and, taking the lead, began to kiss her. Ingrid went along with the program, hoping the Potbelly was watching and would soon get excited enough to join them.

Another door at the head of the bed opened, and the bath lady entered. She nodded to Sue to join her on the bed. Sue stood up, wondering what to do with the needle under her arm, but the decision was quickly made for her.

Potbelly must have observed his fill. He came through the same door, joining the girls. Sue moved into the mix, and while Potbelly was trying to have oral sex with Ingrid, she rolled over surreptitiously and stuck the needle in his inner thigh. He was so engrossed with Ingrid, the needle never phased him. He kept on mauling her as the *sux* began its journey through his bloodstream. When he began to fade, Ingrid pulled his head to her breast to cover his gasping.

He tried to squirm loose, but she had a death grip on him. She motioned the other girls to leave, and for Sue to move closer. It had to appear that they were both doing a number on him.

When Sue was close enough, Ingrid whispered, "The cameras are running, and we have to make it look like he's worn out and wants to rest. We'll hold him between us for a while, then roll him over on his stomach and ease out of bed. He has a past history of falling asleep after he releases. They'll come in before long to wake him. We can use that time to get the hell out of here."

Sue murmured, "The SOB should be dead by now, and he's still breathing. I hope the stuff doesn't have a short shelf life and we're past the killing stage. Shit!"

"Jesus, I hope all this hasn't been for nothing," Ingrid whispered back."

Sue felt the pulse again and said quietly, "We better get going. If he doesn't die, he'll have one hell of a headache, and we don't want to be around when that happens. Maybe one of the guys can snipe him when he leaves the hotel. Let's get."

They rolled him over and slid off the bed, retreating through the same door they'd come through, heading down the empty hallway to the first room, where their clothes were, hoping to change and be gone before he died or woke up with one splitting headache.

When they entered the room where their clothes were, their two escorts from the limo were sitting there waiting to watch them change.

Ignoring them, Sue and Ingrid changed. When the two got up and turned to the door to leave, Sue dropped the one closest to her with a brisk chop to the back of his neck. When the other one turned in surprise, Ingrid hit him over the head with a handy lamp.

With the two guys down, Sue retrieved their pistols and handed one to Ingrid. "Do you know how to use one of these?"

"Not a problem, Sue, I can hit anything close enough to give us trouble. I'm not timid about killing someone trying to kill me."

Using the bodies to block the door, they looked around and found this room had a window facing the side street. Sue tried it, and it opened easily. Quint was watching kitty-corner from the hotel and spotted them right away. He waved to catch their attention and pointed to the guards watching the entrance. They fell in with the confusion on the streets, pushing and shoving their way across to the corner.

"Well, what happened?" Quint was not a happy camper.

Sue responded, her voice betraying her own agitation, "What the hell are you pissed about? We were the ones with our tits in the ringer. I don't know if the fucker died or not. He was still breathing when we left him. It wasn't a good time to hang around to admire our handiwork. The stuff may have outrun its shelf life. I don't know. If he didn't die, he'll come out a side door near where we exited. If we hang out here, we might get a shot at him. Ingrid can go find Jake and Kim, and they can come and pick us up."

"I'm just a little pissed because I didn't like the idea of this operation from the beginning, and it's been going downhill since day one," said Quint. It might not be a good idea to hang around here with all the turmoil. Then again, since you've already taken the risk, we might as well finish the job.

"Ingrid, go find Jake and Kim. We'll be here, hoping to have another opportunity to take out Potbelly if he survived the needle."

"Quint, I don't think we killed the two limo drivers, and they surely have come to by now. When they get together with Potbelly's people, they're going to put two and two together and figure out we weren't the exciting sex objects he expected. I can't believe we're standing here in broad daylight, the only two round-eyes on the street, with a national emergency going on, and no one has hassled us."

Quint retorted, "Well, if he doesn't come out soon, dead or alive, we need to disappear."

It wasn't long before Ingrid returned with Kim and Jake in the Cooper. The Cooper would be cramped, but it was a solid, maneuverable car if a chase was in the cards.

Quint said, "Pull over to the alley. We'll give this confusion another ten minutes; then we're heading back to the trawler."

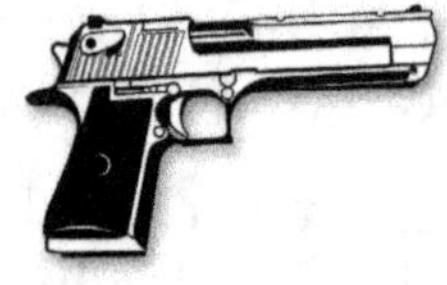

Chapter Eight

Escape

Jake steered the Cooper into the alley and joined Quint and Sue on the corner. "Kim and I have some good news, if we're not mistaken. I think we saw Sunny riding in a little minitruck; it turned down the alley just as I was getting out of the Cooper. There were two in the front and four in the back. A tarp covered the back half of the bed."

"But Sunny was killed in the firefight after the explosion turned the dock area into an inferno."

"Well, that might be what was put out there for our consumption. I have a C-note that says he was in the truck!" retorted Jake.

Before Quint could respond to Jake's bet, Potbelly and his entourage burst out of the side door. Potbelly looked wobbly, supported on either side by large bodyguards. They stepped into the alley just in time to encounter the minitruck. Sunny was driving. He turned the wheel and slammed on the brakes, bringing the truck around with the bed facing the exit door. The guys in the back flipped the tarp off, exposing twin .50 caliber machine guns. The onslaught destroyed Potbelly and his bodyguards, along with the entire wall of the hotel. The smoke hadn't cleared before the building imploded, crashing down in a pile of rubble.

Taking advantage of the confusion from the explosion, Sunny drove across the street. He stopped and yelled out to Quint, "Nice try, Quint. Follow me. You can't go back to the docks. I got word to the captain that the army was going to seize his ship. I told him that I would help you. He shipped out pronto."

The words tailed off as Sunny pointed the truck north, dodging the disarray in the streets. The debris from the explosion had scattered in all directions.

Quint, Sue, and Jake dashed across the street and into what remained of the alley. They piled into the Cooper. Quint yelled out, "Jake, I owe you a hundred. Now get the Cooper in gear. Try to keep up with Sunny; he's our ticket out of here."

As soon as they pulled up behind Sunny, he took off like a madman. After enough turns to make a merry-go-round dizzy, he turned into a narrow, dark alley and disappeared.

Jake pulled the Cooper halfway into the alley and stopped looking around for the minitruck. It was nowhere to be found. "He couldn't have just vanished. Let's get out and search the alley."

The team squeezed out of the little car and started walking the alley, looking for a hidden garage door or anything that looked big enough to hide a truck.

Quint said, "What the hell's going on here? Why would he tell us to follow him and then ditch us?"

They were about to give up the search when Quint's cell barked at him. "Quint here."

Sunny's voice came through the speaker. "Drive the Cooper down to the end of the alley and turn left. You'll see an eighteen-wheeler. Drive up the ramp into the cargo trailer. We had to be sure you weren't being followed. See you."

"Jesus, what a convoluted mess. Get in the Cooper. That was Sunny. Jake, take the Cooper to the end of the alley and make a left. You'll see a semi parked with the trailer ramp down. Drive up the ramp and into the trailer. Let's go!"

Jake popped the clutch and smoked the tires, hitting the brakes in time at the end of the alley to make the left, and the ramp was there as predicted. Once inside, the Cooper barely stopped in time to keep from crashing into the far end of the trailer.

"Geez, Jake, this isn't a destruction derby," remarked Sue. "We have enough trouble without you getting us killed inside a moving morgue."

Two of Sunny's people pulled up the ramp as the semi began to move. One of the men leaned into the window and instructed them to exit the Cooper and take the seats provided in the forward compartment of the trailer.

Quint and Sue led the way through the false wall in the trailer to find a comfortable lounge area. There were seats for ten people, with water and light snacks available.

Quint's cell announced itself again. "Quint here."

"Quint, Sunny. You'll find the quarters a little cramped, but safe for now. We use the trucks to transport political dissidents across the border whenever we can. Maybe with Potbelly out of the picture now we won't have to do our business clandestinely for long.

"Sorry about your attempt and the trawler leaving without you. We have had a plan in progress for some time. We weren't aware of your timing or your exact plans until just before you made your move. We had to wait until you were out of the building. It was our intent to blow the hotel up and blame it on a gas leak. When you showed up, we had to move fast to take advantage of the situation.

Our inside guy called to tell us Potbelly was groggy, but not near death. We delayed the bomb inside and figured to get him when he and his people tried to make their exit to find help for him. It all came out okay in the end. The problem now is that the authorities know it wasn't gas and that Potbelly was gunned down. It will be super hot in the whole country now. Our escape will be a challenge."

Quint asked, "Where are we heading?"

"North."

"China?"

"No, to a coastal city, where the trawler will meet us and you people can get away as planned, only from a different point. Captain Bagmanovich is standing by off the coast waiting for word from us. The coast guard is still on the payroll of Mr. Wing and loyal to him. With Potbelly out of the way and the government overthrown, they'll be in a position to fall in with the new leaders. They'll follow the money until then. We have a long, dangerous trip ahead of us.

"In the compartment above your heads is a cache of weapons in case we need to shoot our way through some checkpoints. We'll travel at night. I have all the documents we need to transport manufactured goods the length of the country. We'll be stopping outside of the city to drop off the Cooper and the minitruck and load up goods for regular delivery. They'll stand close inspection at most checkpoints. See you at the first stop."

Quint closed the cell and relayed the information to the team. Sue remarked, "I don't like being cramped up in this box. We'll be fish in a barrel if things go bad. How about we check out what weapons Sunny has provided for defense or offense, depending on the situation. Hopefully we won't need to shoot our way out. I don't like our chances if the army surrounds a couple of semi-truck trailers full of wanted fugitives."

Jake and Kim pulled a chair under the ceiling compartment above them. Kim opened the hatch to reveal an assortment of firearms that could give them the edge in a ticklish situation.

"Damn. We have plenty of firepower."

The trailer was rocking back and forth in the stop-and-go traffic, making it hard to stand or even sit. Sunny hadn't said how long it would be before they would stop to drop the vehicles and pick up the freight.

Sue, still not in favor of the confinement, said, "By the looks of this operation, it's not Sunny's first rodeo. His operation is fine-tuned, and we've put our complete faith in him. What if he's not what he seems? We could be on our way to the local hoosegow."

Quint retorted, "Sue, I spent some harrowing times with Sunny, and I'm willing to put my life on the line for him, as he did for me. No worries about his loyalty or intentions."

Their banter was interruped as the truck made a sudden stop, sending them all tumbling to the bed of the trailer. Before they could get to their feet, they heard the rear doors open. Then the false door opened and there stood Sunny, laughing at the sight of them trying to get to their feet.

He stepped into the compartment and gave Quint, Jake, and Kim big bear hugs. Turning to Sue, he said, "This must be the super-snooper you guys are always bragging on. Hello, Sue. I don't think we've met. And this must be Ingrid. You have a good team here, Quint. I've been getting reports on your activities, and my sources are better than the late Potbelly's."

One glance at Sue, and Quint could see she was having seconds thoughts about Sunny. Her expression had changed to one of approval.

"Our escape is now more dangerous than ever. This will be one of many stops and layovers as we work our way north.

"The exchange of the vehicles for the cargo is under-way, and we'll be safe here until dark. I have an advance party leading the way. They'll give us a call when it's time to move out. I'll get back to you after dark, when I return from a little recon up the highway," Sunny said as he disappeared, and a couple of his people backed the Cooper out of the trailer, while others prepared to load the false cargo for the journey north.

Sue and Quint stood near the rear ramp as Sunny's team loaded the cargo. She said, "I think we're putting ourselves in a moving coffin. We won't have a chance if we're stopped. It would be better to walk all the way and be able to disperse in five directions. At least they would have to split their forces five ways, and one or more of us would be able to escape."

Quint looked at Sue with admiration. She possessed not only beauty, but also panache. She was a clear thinker with loads of common sense, a great lover, and a fighter. What more could a guy ask for? "I agree, Sue. We need to have a sit down with Sunny and figure another way to get the hell out of here. But let's come up with something before we step on his plan."

Kim and Jake, wanting to avoid further banter, took cover in the secret compartment of the truck trailer.

Ingrid, never one to back off, suggested, "The sea is our best way out of this predicament. I think we should call the captain and ask him to find a suitable place to meet that is not far from where we are now. He's a wizard in these waters, and we'll find our way to that part of the coast. But let's get it squared away with the captain before Sunny comes back. We can tell him where we need to go and share our opinions with him."

Quint looked over at Sue, who nodded her head in agreement and said, "Sounds good to me."

Jake and Kim stuck their heads out of the compartment and chimed in at the same time, "Let's go with the nearest beach."

Quint flipped the cell phone open and punched in the captain's number. "Captain, this is Quint. We're in a bit of trouble here, since things didn't go well with the hit. Sunny wants to take us north in a couple of semi trailers, but we'd rather take our chances finding something a little closer than he has in mind. Do you have any suggestions on how we can make that happen?"

"You know, Quint, you guys are becoming a real pain in the ass. I just barely made it out of the harbor before the army got to the docks. It's a good thing Mr. Wing has the coast guard in his pocket. But if you can find your way to the port of Sanwo, I can put in there for a day, no more.

"It'll take me a few days to go around the tip and motor up. You should be able to go almost straight across from where you are. Not nearly as far as I'll have to travel. You'll be there long before I arrive, so plan on staying out of sight for a couple of days. Let me know what you're going to do. I'm heading that way anyway—fishing's not bad up there."

Quint was about to ask a few questions when the cell went dark. He put the cell in its holster, smiled at the group, and relayed what the captain had suggested. "I like it. Not so far to go, and the only hang-up is hiding out for a couple of days in the port city. Sunny shouldn't be put out by a shorter trip, with all his excess baggage."

It was nearly dark when Sunny approached the trailer and climbed in. He was about to say something when Quint said, "Sunny, we need to have a chat about the planned trip north."

Sunny wasn't smiling when he replied, "No need to worry about that, Quint. I have received some bad news from my source in the government. Potbelly's people got wind of an attempt on his life about the time you and I were putting our plans into play. They didn't know of your plan or mine, but it put them on the alert. Potbelly sent in a substitute at the hotel. The guy sure looked like him, but we dusted an imposter. It was all for nothing, other than killing some of his henchmen. But all may not be lost."

Quint retorted, "What do you mean, all is not lost? We fucking killed the wrong guy. Shit!"

"Listen, Quint. The informant said that after Potbelly got the news of the attempt, he fled to his yacht. He's lying a couple of miles off the coast, afraid to come ashore. We might have a chance to sink his sorry ass while he's still out there and blame it on the weather or something."

Sue chimed in, "He'll have an armada around his yacht. How the hell would we get to him?"

"Too bad we don't have a jet to take him out," Jake remarked.

Kim joined in, "How often do you get information from inside the administration?"

Sunny, standing tall near the rear of the trailer, made the doorway look small. He answered, "Not as often as we'd like, but every couple of days some news slips through the cracks. Sometimes it's our guy, other times reliable rumor. We're going to take the truck and trailers back into the city, where we have a compound that is fairly safe. Nothing here is a hundred percent, as you know."

Quint put his hand up to quiet the chatter. "I'm going to give the captain another call and explain the situation. Maybe he'll have some idea how to tackle the yacht and its armada of protection. By the way, Sunny, do you think we have a leak on our end—yours, or Mr. Wing's?"

Sunny's usually smiling face abruptly changed to an ugly snarl. "I don't know. They might have just played it safe, not having confirmed info, but if there is a leak on my end, whoever dropped the dime on us will be dead the minute they are exposed. I'll get the trucks turned around while you call the captain. Let's get the show on the road, as you say in the States." He jumped down and started ordering the drivers to turn the semis around.

When the trucks pulled out onto the unkept blacktop highway, Sue got that tingle in the back of her neck that always spells trouble. "Quint, I have that feeling of doom. We might just bag this whole thing and escape with our bodies in one piece. This thing has gone downhill from the getgo."

Quint replied, "Have you ever thrown in the towel on a mission before?"

"Quint, I'm not begging off for no good reason. There comes a time when it looks like it wasn't meant to be. I've never given up before, and at the same time, I've never been involved in such a clusterfuck before. Ingrid and I survived some serious shit, only to bag the wrong game. Sunny and his crew blew up a hotel and killed how many people? There's only one good thing that's come out of this mess so far—we're not dead."

"Well, I think you should put your doubts on the back burner, turn down the flame, and lighten up. Join in the effort to finish the job."

"Don't jump to conclusions, Quint. I'm not quitting. I want that fucker as bad as anyone else. I'm just venting, and you're handy."

Sue turned away and took a seat in the secret compartment. Quint shook his head. *I'll never understand women. Damn, they can be the best part or the worst part of a day.*

The trailers swayed with the rough road, slowing down and speeding up, depending on the conditions. The drivers made good time, heading for the compound.

At the first pit stop, Quint asked the driver if he could ride shotgun in the tractor. The man was more than happy to have company and gave Quint his automatic rifle in case they had trouble at one of the checkpoints.

After they had been rolling for a while, they stopped briefly at the first checkpoint, passing through without incident. Quint radioed the trailer, "Jake, do you read me? The driver says we may have trouble at the next checkpoint. The guards were suspicious when we came through earlier, and we'll be doubly suspect coming back so soon. Lock and load everything you have back there, and if I signal you, get the hell out of that coffin. Come out shooting!"

"Ten-four, Quint."

As they approached the second checkpoint, Sunny, in the lead truck, talking into the handheld radio, gave a description. "The checkpoint has been reinforced with more soldiers and larger weapons. We'll blast our way through, abandon the trucks, and disappear into the city. The compound is not far. We can make it there on foot once we're through the checkpoint.

"We'll have to eliminate everyone manning the checkpoint, and surprise will be our best weapon when the festivities begin. I'm going to jackknife the rig and slide sideways into the guard shack. Quint, bring your tractor and trailer straight in, exit the rear, and take out the guards on our flanks. We'll take out what's left in the shack and the reserves behind it."

Quint could see the guard shack at the end of the block. He asked Jake, "Did you get that radio call from Sunny?"

"Yeah, he came in loud and clear. We're ready to exit and engage."

"Good. One block to go, pal. Soon as we stop, take out anything within range; don't worry about collateral damage. We're going to be lucky to survive this, so don't be shy."

Quint had just clicked the radio off when he saw the truck in front slam on its brakes and begin its long slide sideways into the guard shack.

Tracer bullets from the cab sprayed the shack and beyond. Soldiers scattered in every direction, trying to outrun the jackknifed truck sliding into their barriers and building. Their return fire was haphazard at best, with most of the bullets going into the street, ricocheting back at the shooter, or shooting skyward.

With all the confusion in full force, it occurred to Quint that Sunny hadn't told them where the compound was. Jumping from the tractor, he and the driver concentrated their fire to the port flank. The crash of Sunny's truck had put out the lights, giving them cover but limited vision. The tracer rounds and muzzle flashes helped them direct their fire.

Quint was hoping for a lull in the gunfight so he could ask the driver where the compound was, but it was not to be. The driver, who had been standing next to him at the front of the tractor, slumped over and dropped to the pavement. He had been hit in the forehead, dead before he hit the street.

As Quint turned to join the others at the trailer's rear door, he saw Sue jerk to one side and fall to the blacktop. His heart skipped a beat as he ran to help her, with the sporadic fire from the guards slowing down as Jake, Kim, Sunny, and his people slowly but surely put out the fire.

Sue was conscious, and she was not a happy camper. When Quint got to her side, she was yelling in disgust, "God damned lucky fucking shot. How the hell could anyone see anything, let alone hit something, in these conditions? It's almost pitch dark. Jesus! It must have been a stray round with my name on it. Shit!"

"Who the hell are you talking to, Sue? Where are you hit?"

"I'm just venting again, Quint. You just happen to be the sounding board. I'm hit in the right side. Just below the breast. You should be able to find the wound blindfolded. It won't be your first time in the area. Now, would you mind getting me to my feet and see where the hell the bullet went?"

Quint suggested, "You might save your energy and help me get your ass out of the line of fire. And don't scare the shit out of me again. Damn, what a beauty you are when you're angry, hurt, and need assistance. Nice to see you have the capacity to accept help. It must be a real pain to show your vulnerable side."

"Quint, savor the moment. It won't happen again, I assure you. Now let's get it done."

They hobbled their way behind the trailer, to find Jake, Ingrid, Kim, and another man running back to join them. The shooting had stopped, and Sunny had sent one of his people to lead them to the compound.

Jake yelled, "We have to follow this guy, *now*! Damn, Sue, you're supposed to zigzag!"

Kim grabbed Sue's left arm, and he and Quint lifted her off her feet and started running following their guide. Jake and Ingrid gave them covering fire as the few enemy who hadn't been killed or wounded found their backbones and started firing again. As they ran past the burning trucks and guard shack, the fuel tanks exploded, knocking them all to the ground. The firing from the guards stopped. They had taken the brunt of the explosion.

With their heads pounding and ears ringing, they managed to get back to their feet and continue their run for the secret compound. Sue was trying to keep a stiff upper lip and be the tough guy, but she faded into unconsciousness, which made it easier for them to carry her, not having to think about her pain.

The streets were jammed with cars, motorcycles, bikes, and people fleeing from the gunfight and explosions. The crowds gave them the opportunity to blend in and disappear into the chaos, with Sue's limp figure not attracting any attention.

They had run three blocks when Sunny's guide stopped at a double-gated block wall and rang the buzzer. After a short conversation, one side of the gate opened enough for them to scamper into a huge open compound. There were buildings in the center, housing for the occupants off to one side, and garage facilities around the perimeter.

As they approached the main building, Sunny came out to meet them. He had a doctor with him. Nodding at the unconscious Sue, Sunny said, "We'll take her to my quarters."

Sunny led them to a modest one-room building. Quint placed Sue gently on the bed. Coming around, Sue asked, "Where are we?"

Quint leaned over and whispered in her ear, "Nice to see you back. I've had fun tending to your wound during our dangerous escape from the burning trucks. I'm happy to see that your I-can-handle-it attitude seems to have taken a vacation."

Sue was starting to fade again, but managed to say, "Don't get used to it, pal; it won't last long, and it will not happen again, I assure you." There was a smile on her angelic face as she drifted into the darkness again.

After a short inspection of the wound, the doctor said, "The bullet went clean through, not hitting anything of importance. She should heal up fine. In the meantime, she'll be in a lot of pain in the area of the wound. I'll give her a shot for now and leave some pain pills for later."

While the doctor was dressing the wound, Sue returned to the world, wincing from the poking and jabbing, "What the hell are you guys doing? Damn! That hurts. I hope everyone had a nice view of my upper body. How about some privacy?"

The doctor put the last of the bandages on, and Ingrid pulled the sheet up to her neck. Sue was about to complain again about something or other, but the shot suddenly took effect, and she disappeared into a comfortable slumber. Ingrid sat down on the bed beside her and held her hand. "I'll take it from here," she said softly.

Sunny announced, "We can't leave the compound for at least a day and a night to allow the worst of the confusion to dissipate. They'll tire of looking for us and get back to some kind of routine. Then we'll take another shot at Potbelly. According to my sources, he's still out there on his yacht, and with tonight's disturbance he'll be more paranoid than before. He's a sitting duck—if we can get to him. Maybe Sue will be well enough by then to be in on the action."

"Captain, how close are you to our objective?" Quint asked.

"I'm near the picket line they have set up around his yacht. Fortunately, no sign of the coast guard. We'll have to create some kind of diversion. I'll think about it. When will you be heading out this way?"

"One day and night here, then we can join you."

Quint closed the cell, and the team gathered to plan the hit on Potbelly. "Sunny, the captain is nearly in position to help. He said the yacht is well protected, and not by the coast guard, but regular navy and some privateers. We'll need a huge diversion to get anywhere near the yacht."

"Not to worry, Quint," Sunny replied. "One of the privateers is under my command. I've had him on standby for three years now, hoping for just this situation to come up. Thanks to you guys putting the heat on, we have a great opportunity to deep six the asshole.

"We have to decide how the attack should go. Let's put something together and run it by Captain Bagmanovich. He has an enormous background in such matters, and he's also got a lot at stake. This action will certainly put his fishing career in jeopardy, maybe even sink his trawler."

Jake, listening to the banter, suggested, "Sunny, do you have access to a boat large enough for us all to take a little cruise out to your man on the picket line? And can we leave a few of your people behind to blow up the docks after we shove off? We could hook up with your people and the captain. Among the three boats, we should be able to take out a yacht! What kind of firepower does your man have?"

"He has a couple of fifties, two mortars, and some rocket-propelled grenades. Plus some AK-47s and sidearms. The fifties could do some real damage, and an accurate mortar or two would help. The RPGs are old and unreliable, and the fifty ammo is old too. It will be an experiment in terror on both sides with the suspect ammo. Click is not a good sound to hear in a gunfight. Nothing is new in this part of the world under the short fuck's dictatorship."

Jake responded, "Well, I think if your guy and our boat could keep the navy busy, the captain could sneak in, ram the yacht, and sink her. His trawler could withstand a good ramming. When he slices through the yacht, we all head for open water and disappear. Piece of cake!"

Kim threw in his two cents. "I think one of us should hang around and make sure the yacht sinks with all hands and the fat fuck on board. It would be a shame to let him off the hook again. It'll be pitch dark out there, except for the spotlights coming from the navy, but with the rough seas, they won't be a problem.

"I checked the weather forecast for the next three days, and it's going to be nasty. We might not even have to do shit. The seas may take him to his reward."

"If the weather is a factor, we'll be in the same boat as they are, so to speak," remarked Quint wryly. "It would be to our benefit for the high seas to take the blame for his disappearance. The captain could still slice through the yacht, and no one would know the difference. Let's get our asses out there and be in position to take advantage of any opportunity that comes our way.

"The yacht's crew will get the same weather report we get. But they won't come ashore if we blow the dock again. I'll get that going. We have tonight and all day tomorrow to rig things up.

"I'll start on that immediately," Sunny said. He headed for the door to give his guys a heads-up on blowing the docks again and fixing up an old fishing boat with some firepower to divert the navy away from Potbelly.

Quint's cell barked. "Quint here. Yes sir." He closed the cell. "Captain Bagmanovich is in position. He's looking for gale-force winds tomorrow night. Good time to strike."

Sunny heard Quint and yelled through the door, "We'll be ready by then."

"How long was I out?" Sue asked, as Quint helped her with another spoon of soup; putting the spoon down, he picked up a cup of hot tea. "Here, sip this," he said. As she took a drink, he explained, "You've been out since the doc gave you a shot last night. It's nearly dark again, so you've been out sixteen-plus hours. By all appearances, your pain seems to have come down to tolerable levels. Will you be up for some open-water adventure? We're going to strike the yacht tonight."

Sue sat forward suddenly. Quint had to move the teacup quickly to avoid spilling the hot tea.

"Hell, yes! You think you can leave me here to sulk, while you guys finish the job? Not a chance, Bucko! Get my clothes and leave me alone to dress. I'll be okay for this."

Sue stood up and then sat down quickly. She didn't appear to be in much pain, so Quint retrieved her clothes and turned his back while she dressed.

Damn, what a woman! She's as exciting wounded as whole, maybe more so. It was nice to assist her without competition for once. But that's over. She's back in warrior mode now.

Quint filled Sue in as she dressed. "Sunny is getting a fishing boat for us to use, and the trawler is in position to strike. The weather is in our favor. You better have your sea legs, for the seas will be turbulent. We might get lucky—the high seas might do the job for us."

"Okay, I'm ready."

When Quint and Sue emerged from Sunny's quarters, the others were waiting in two trucks. The large fishing boat that Sunny had fixed up for the coming battle with the navy and the high seas would be waiting for them at the dock. Sunny's privateer and the fishing boat would distract the navy and other privateers while the captain sliced the yacht in two. The wind and the rough surf would make it a tough job.

As they approached the marina area, conditions were already worsening. Waves were breaking over the docks, making it risky to board the fishing boat, let alone head her out to sea. Sunny, his sea legs working well on the bow of the boat, yelled, "Come on, we don't have much time. Get aboard so we can cast off."

Easier said than done—the boat was rocking in every direction from the crashing waves. Quint yelled up to Sunny, "You think this might be a little too good? Shit, this is big-time badass weather!"

"Get aboard; we won't have a chance like this again. The yacht will be a sitting duck, with the navy worried about their own asses, not just Potbelly's."

Quint and Jake helped Sue and Ingrid aboard, while Kim stood ready to cast off the bow and stern lines.

When Sunny gave the word, Kim let loose the lines just as the fishing boat caught a swell that made it impossible for Kim to board. They pulled away from the dock as he waved frantically for them to come back. That wasn't possible. Kim was left behind to help Sunny's men blow the docks.

Sunny's temporary man-of-war didn't have the size needed to combat the waves, let alone a navy blockade around a yacht. The swells were enormous and the winds treacherous, sending the little boat up and down like a fishing-line bob. Most of the team were hanging on for dear life, as the captain of the small craft enjoyed the misery of the landlubbers. He smiled, steering her into the wind as huge white-caps broke over the bow, soaking the ship from stem to stern.

The captain of the fishing vessel knew that not too far out into the gulf, the weather was better, not nearly as harsh as near the coastline. He didn't share that information, not wanting to spoil the fun.

Quint yelled above the noise of the storm, "We might have a problem making war in this weather! Our only hope is that the yacht sinks by itself."

Sunny, leaning into the wind, remarked, "Not to worry, Quint. The weather is better a little further out. Not much, but enough to allow us to get the job done. The captain will guide us to our destination regardless of the conditions."

Sue and Ingrid were below trying to keep from heaving all over the deck. Sue's wound wasn't high on her list of ailments at the present time. She'd never been seasick before, and she'd assumed she never would be, but this turbulence made her rethink her yearning for any sea duty.

Jake was of the same mind as the captain, having a great time at the expense of the others. He had always been a good sailor, and a little weather didn't deter him from enjoying the voyage.

Quint, you look a little green," he said with a smile and a wink.

Captain Bagmanovich had brought the trawler close enough to the picket line to receive a radio message warning him to change course or be fired upon. He changed course, looking for Sunny's privateer. The weather was so bad it would be hard to connect with the good guys so they could give him the opening he needed.

Using his cell, the captain contacted Sunny. "Tell your privateer guy to give me three shorts and a long from his spotlight. It's too rough here for me to single him out. Where are you now?"

"We're not far off. When you see the docks explode, we'll be a short distance from the privateer and visible to you as we hit the peak of the swells. He'll pull out of the way and head for the nearest navy ship to start a battle. We'll do the same, drawing them to us while you sail in and split the yacht in half."

"Ten-four." The captain closed the cell and scanned the horizon, looking for the floodlight signal from the privateer.

Quint and Jake made their way up to the bridge to assist the crew searching for their privateer contact. Sunny, too, was on the bridge, calling Kim to let him know it was time to blow the docks. He'd just closed the cell when the docks lit up the sky, and their privateer's floodlights began going on and off like neon signs on the Las Vegas Strip. His distress signal should draw the closest navy vessel to his aid. He motored out of the picket line, allowing an opening for Captain Bagmanovich.

Quint had been looking back at the dock area when the night sky turned to daylight for a few seconds, blinding him and the others who had turned to watch."

"Whoa! What the hell did they blow up?" asked Jake as he tried to get his night vision back.

Quint replied, "I don't know, but I hope they were far enough away and didn't go up with it." The boat captain pointed into the darkness as Sunny's privateer pulled out of the picket line, and when the swells were just right, the trawler could be seen heading through the vacated area.

The yacht wasn't visible, but they were closing fast in the rough seas, and it wouldn't be long before a navy ship would challenge them with a shot across the bow. When the navy ship was distracted, Captain Bagmanovich would steer for the yacht.

The ship-to-ship radio began to crackle and pop, and then the voice of Captain Bagmanovich came over loud and clear, as he spoke in his native Russian.

Jake yelled, "Ingrid, we need you up here on the bridge. The trawler is speaking your language so the Zazakurens won't understand."

Ingrid, holding back the urge to fill another bag, raced up to the bridge in time to pass along what Bagmanovich was saying. She relayed the message as he spoke, gagging on every other word, but controlling the urge to vomit from the seasickness.

"Quint, Sunny, whoever can hear me. I have a visual on the yacht. It appears in between swells. There is a navy vessel heading my way, but I think I can beat him to Potbelly.

"I'll slice through his yacht; then I'll make a hard turn to starboard and head due south at flank speed. Maybe I can outrun the used-up old navy ship. He looks slow and lumbering."

Quint was looking through his binoculars at the unfolding events, dead ahead of their position. When the fishing boat peaked on a swell, he could see the trawler on course to split the yacht in two. The navy ship was on an interception course. The trawler was closer, though, and it would hit the yacht before the navy ship could intercede.

There was a flash from the navy vessel's guns as it bore down on the yacht and trawler, but it didn't hit anything.

Quint yelled into the ship-to-ship radio, "The navy vessel is bearing down on you, but it looks good for you to hit pay dirt first. We'll try and draw the navy towards us as you make your way south. They'll have to choose which one of us to chase. We're smaller, so they might well challenge us and leave you be."

Before Quint had finished, the rough seas briefly opened, allowing them to see the trawler slice the yacht into two pieces, sending them to the bottom in seconds. There was no chance of survivors.

The navy ship fired its cannon again, taking a shot in the dark. As luck would have it, the round landed on the trawler and went through the bridge structure without exploding until it hit the stern fishing reels. It missed the bridge crew by inches, but two sailors who were re-rigging the reels because of the high seas were killed instantly.

Captain Bagmanovich's heading was now due south at flank speed. The old navy ship couldn't keep up and veered off to take on the smaller fishing vessel.

Sunny thought the fishing captain was reacting a little slowly to the advancing navy ship and remarked, "Well, captain, we've managed to accomplish our goal. You do see the ship coming our way? They are armed and much bigger than our little fishing boat. Do you suppose it would be prudent to get the fuck out of the way?"

The captain assumed a look of utter amazement at Sunny's words. He retorted, "You obviously are not much of a sailor, or you would notice that the navy ship is having a terrible time with the huge swells. The ship's captain is not experienced in this weather. They'll swamp before they reach us."

Sunny, not knowing what to say, just nodded.

While everyone was focused on the navy ship coming their way, an explosion rocked the boat. A round from a privateer to the northwest hit the stern of the boat. The captain immediately brought the boat around, trying to head her into the oncoming privateer. The second round went across the bow as he came about. He then steered directly at the other boat and pushed the throttles to full-ahead. The game of chicken had begun.

The privateer gave no sign of veering off.

Jake, Quint, and Sunny were on the bridge, none of them looking forward to a game of chicken on the high seas, when the captain yelled out, "We'll find our target directly to our front when we peak on the next roller."

He was correct: as they came crashing down from the deep swell, they missed the other boat by inches. The captain brought the boat around again, putting them on a heading for the docks. With a sigh of relief, Quint motioned the others to join him below.

They had just slid down the ladder to below decks, when there was a huge explosion from above. Quint, the last one down the ladder, climbed back up to see what the hell had happened.

Shortly, he yelled back down to the others, "The bridge took a direct hit. The captain and all steering capabilities are gone. The crew has abandoned ship. I suggest we all grab life jackets and whatever weaponry is available and jump ship. There's a regular navy ship on our stern that we didn't see when the privateer passed us. The navy ship has all the cannon they need to blow us out of the water. The boat is going to either swamp without a helm, or the navy will sink us. Come on! Let's get the fuck out of here!"

Jake grabbed Sue and helped her up the ladder, followed by Sunny and Ingrid. They had precious little time to get off the fishing boat before their worst nightmare came to pass.

Another round hit the bow of the boat as they tried to jump off the port side. Sunny managed to throw Ingrid off before he was swept overboard and lost from sight.

Jake and Quint held onto Sue as they were washed off the deck into the swirling sea. It was pure luck that Ingrid was within reach and they could lock arms to keep together.

Their stay in the cold water wouldn't be long. The navy vessel was upon them in minutes. The captain had the crew let go a burst of machine gun fire to establish who had the upper hand.

Chapter Eight
Escape

The wind and the swells died down as quickly as they'd come up, and a rescue boat was launched to pick them up.

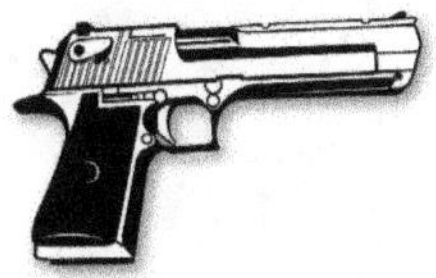

Chapter Nine

Captured

The calming sea gave them a chance for rescue, but it was a two-edged sword. They might drown or succumb to the cold water, but then again the launch coming their way might just shoot them. Rescue by the enemy might not be their best bet.

"Everyone check your weapons," ordered Quint. "If they appear to intend us harm instead of rescue, let's give them all we have. Kinda like a mouse giving the finger to an eagle as he swoops down."

The only weapons the team had were handguns carried into the water as they were washed off the fishing boat. They would be outgunned against the firepower of the automatic rifles that were sure to be carried by the launch headed toward them.

Sue and Ingrid were getting their sea legs just in time to be in a gun battle that they couldn't possibly win—or be captured.

"Where's Sunny?" asked Sue.

Jake was the first to respond. "When he helped Ingrid off the boat, the waves took him over the off side, and he disappeared in the swells. His chances for survival are not good. Here comes the launch. Damn, we're in for it now."

"What's he saying?" asked Quint, as the launch drifted within arm's reach.

"His English sucks, and he seems uncertain what to do with us," responded Jake. "We aren't the ones who sank the yacht, but they did fire on us and sink the fishing boat. I think we should just try to cooperate. If they were going to shoot us, that would've happened already."

Quint nodded and remarked, "They'll want to pump us for all the information they can get about our involvement with the sinking. Soon as they realize we're all round eyes, the shit will hit the fan. Damn! We're in one tight-ass situation."

The sailors threw a rescue ring to Sue and motioned for her to put it around her waist so they could pull her aboard the launch. She looked over at Jake and Quint for some sign of resistance, as she started to pull her handgun.

Quint said, "Keep the pistol hidden as long as possible. We might be able to sneak something by them. They are sailors, not trained soldiers."

Sue nodded, put her arms through the ring, slipped it over her head, and the men aboard the launch pulled her out of the water. The sailors were getting excited about capturing a round-eyed woman. They were jabbering and pointing at her, and then at the others in the water.

The one who seemed to be in charge yelled excitedly into his radio as the crew pulled the rest of the team aboard. He was about to burst with his good fortune to be the one who captured the Western infidels.

They were sloppy searching the wet bodies, and overlooked the guns on Sue and Ingrid.

They patted down Jake and Quint with more care and discovered their handguns, taking pleasure in being rough with them.

With everyone aboard, the launch came about and headed back to the mother ship. The weather had started to turn bad again.

Quint cautioned the others in a low voice, "No talking. When the opportunity presents itself, we'll try to escape. Ingrid, it would be best if they don't discover you're Russian."

The launch pulled alongside the ship, and the deck-hands used pulleys to bring her aboard. The captain was standing on deck yelling orders in every direction as Quint stepped on deck.

There was an interpreter next to the captain, and he said to Quint, "The captain wants to know the name of the fishing boat, its port of call, the owner, and what you were doing in these waters."

Quint retorted, "We rented the fishing boat in China for a weekend of fishing."

The interpreter repeated his answer, and the captain turned bright red and barked an order at his guards. They moved forward and struck Quint numerous times on his back and legs, knocking him to the deck.

The beady-eyed captain ranted for a good five minutes, before his words were translated to the four soaked, shivering captives.

"Our beloved leader's yacht was attacked by a Russian trawler. The ship sliced the yacht in half, with all hands lost. The leader of this great country is dead, and I think you round-eyed, evil, capitalist pigs had a hand in it. When we return to shore, the army will have a field day with you, and the Russian trawler will be run down and destroyed."

The interpreter continued, "He would kill you now, but for the pleasure of watching you tortured by the army professionals. Your government won't be able to help you. It's not often the killer is caught red-handed."

The captain turned and rattled off some unintelligible gibberish as they were taken below decks and shackled to the sleeping racks in the crew's quarters. One sailor stayed behind to keep an eye on the enchained captives.

"Sue, do you still have your handgun?" Quint asked in a low voice.

Sue squirmed. It was very uncomfortable with her hands wrapped around the steel rack post.

"Yes, it's still between my legs. Don't you dare come up with any wiseass remarks. At least we're armed."

Ingrid chimed in. "I still have mine too. I learned where to hide a small handgun while I was at the mercy of the old Soviet Union soldiers. It saved my life more than once. I sure would like to move it to a more comfortable position."

Jake had a big smile on his face. "Ladies, you give new meaning to the term 'heater.'" They were all smiling at that one when the other crew members came back, and the slapping and hitting began in earnest, the questions coming at a rapid pace.

The only English-speaking one in the group said, "You people are from the West, and you wear no uniforms, so you must be spies. The penalty for spying is death, which will happen to you as soon as we turn you over to the army."

Quint tried to tell motormouth that they were civilians who had rented the fishing boat for a weekend of deep-sea fishing. Due to the storm they had gotten lost, and would they please release them, put them ashore, and find them transportation back to China? He was rewarded with a swift kick in the rib cage.

Motormouth focused most of his physical abuse on Quint and Jake, apparently not knowing how to handle the two women, so he limited them to verbal abuse. They would be in deep shit if any visible marks were left on any of them, which would make it impossible to use them for propaganda purposes, the tool of the communists since television began to be widely viewed throughout the world.

The abuse stopped as suddenly as it had started when the ship cut power, and the voice of the captain came over the ship's intercom.

They couldn't understand what the captain was saying, but it appeared the deckhands were getting ready to dock the ship as they bolted up the stairwell. Their picnic was about to end. The army wouldn't be so easy on the four round-eyed intruders.

Quint said, "We keep the rented fishing boat story. They can't prove we didn't come from China, since the navy destroyed the evidence."

Jake said, "The army will do a detailed search of our persons. The guns will be discovered. If we intend to use them, it has to be before the army gets their hands on us."

"If we don't get a chance to make a break for it, Sue, you and Ingrid ditch the handguns at the first opportunity, before we get a final inspection," Quint said.

Ingrid shrugged her shoulders and leaned her head towards the open hatch. "Here they come."

The squawk box finally shut down when the ship bumped into the dock and came to a stop. Motormouth was giving orders to release the round-eyes, grinning with the prospect of helping the army torture the trespassers. His sadistic side shined through his well-mannered appearance.

The sailors released their bonds and hustled them topside, poking with their rifles, taking their last chance to vent their anger.

As they reached the deck, they saw the massive damage to the port facilities. There was nothing standing that hadn't been touched by the explosion. Kim and the others had certainly made an impression on the landscape. Everything within eyesight was charred and twisted. Whatever commerce had been warehoused waiting to be loaded, or on ships in the port was utterly devastated. The dock area was a disaster.

They were marched down the gangway and loaded onto an old U.S. Army truck, left over from the last war. They were lashed to the bench seats running down each side of the truck's bed and to each other. There were guards at the end of each bench.

Quint leaned toward the others and murmured, "Our only chance may be to take the truck down before we get to a prison or army post. We'll wait and see what they have following us. Damn, look at the army; they're swarming the ship."

Single shots could be heard from below decks and automatic fire swept the topside. The ship was being purged for some reason or another. Everyone left on board was eliminated. Whoever had taken the dictator's place didn't want any witnesses to the sinking of the yacht.

"I don't like the look of this, guys. If they're willing to kill the whole crew of a navy ship, our chances aren't worth spit," said Jake as they watched the carnage.

Kim and Sunny's guerrillas were gathered in the compound discussing their next move to keep the pressure on while there was so much confusion in the port city. The word had come from their spy planted inside army headquarters that Potbelly's yacht had capsized in the storm off the coast, all hands going down with the boat.

Kim smiled at the news. Sunny had hit his mark. The dictator was dead, and they had a chance to take the country into the twenty-first century, with the will of the people deciding the form of government.

But the spy hadn't finished his report. He added that four westerners had been captured at sea and were now on their way to the main prison. There were two women and two men.

This unexpected news turned Kim's stomach. He would have to get down to the prison to see for himself if it was his teammates or someone else who had stumbled into a bad situation. He jumped into the minitaxi they used for a disguise, telling the driver to head for the prison near the army headquarters. He wanted to get there before the army truck described by the spy took the prisoners inside the walls.

The cab sped into the heavy traffic, dodging any number of near collisions. Kim gave the driver kudos for his skills and suggested he could drive on the NASCAR circuit in the States.

They parked the cab at the top of a hill overlooking the prison, just in time to see the army truck coming up the crowded street towards the main gate.

Kim told the driver to take the cab down to the street and cause an accident with the truck. He wanted the truck to be unloaded outside the gate so he could see who the four roundeyes were. If it was Quint and the gang, he would begin planning a prison break.

Kim got out of the cab and stood on the hill. He watched as the driver navigated the narrow street and crashed the cab into the vehicle in front of the truck, which plowed into the rear of the car. A traffic jam immediately formed.

The confusion spread in both directions. Army guards from the prison came out the front gate in full force to restore order, but were in conflict with the police, who had arrived to take charge. In the end, the truck was surrounded by the soldiers, and the four prisoners were helped down to the street.

Kim's heart sank. He saw his friends, hands tied behind them, blindfolded, and herded like sheep through the front gate. If he'd had some people there, it would have been an ideal time to strike. He wondered what happened to Sunny. He watched as the cab driver slipped away from the accident scene, leaving the stolen cab a mystery to the police.

Kim hailed another cab, returning to a spot a few blocks from the compound and walking the rest of the way as he thought about how to proceed with the prison break and wondering again what happened to Sunny. He would be hard-pressed to put together a force big enough to attack the prison, but having support from inside could turn the tide in their favor.

Chapter Ten

Breakout

Safely within the compound, Kim gathered Sunny's people together and asked, "Do we have anyone working in the prison next to army headquarters who can help us with inside information? We have four freedom fighters jailed there, and we need to break them out. It won't be easy for a number of reasons, but one in particular is that they are Westerners, a prize collected by those who hope to take the deceased Potbelly's position of power. When the news of the yacht sinking gets worldwide attention, they'll use the four prisoners as the culprits who assassinated the beloved leader of the communist state. Extra security will surround them. We'll have to be very clever to gain their freedom."

A lone hand appeared in the rear. "My son is a guard on the night shift at the prison. He works in the warden's office." The hand belonged to a mama-san who had worked in the compound since Sunny had put his force together to free his people from the yoke of the communism.

"Would you please step forward?' Kim asked. The old woman moved at a snail's pace through the crowd with her head down, not looking at anyone.

When she stood in front of Kim, she looked up, smiled, and with eyes as bright as a teenager, said, "My name is Mary Soso. I have been with Sunny since his first day here. I clean the office building and do what I can to free our people. My son, David Soso, will help us from his position inside the prison."

Kim, looking down at Mary, saw a frail, gray-haired woman in her winter years, a woman with the enthusiasm of a person thirty years her junior. Her jawline revealed a woman determined to make their world a better place and leave a legacy of freedom for her grandchildren. Her bright eyes and smile nearly brought Kim to tears. *If everyone in the country had her grit and soul, the evil would be expelled from here in short order.*

"Mary, how often do you see your son?"

"He still lives at home. I can communicate anything you wish."

"Does David sit in a position of authority?"

"Yes, he is the night shift supervisor for the guards."

"Mary, how did you come by your Christian name?"

"I was raised in a Catholic orphanage. I'm at your service, Mr. Kim, and I say prayers every night for the soul of Sunny. I haven't seen him in so long. Do you know what happened to him?"

"We don't know for sure. He may have been lost at sea fighting for the goal of freedom that you have given your long life to."

"I will pray twice tonight: that the sea gives Sunny up and that he returns to help us once again in our struggle."

She smiled at Kim, gave him a wink, and returned to her position in the rear as the crowd separated, giving her a wide path, feeling humble in her presence.

Kim was speechless, thinking of her as a saint sent to help them overcome the odds. God works in mysterious ways, especially in a communist-dominated society. He then dismissed the group, with the exception of the officers, who stayed for a planning session.

"Ladies and gentlemen, with all the confusion that will beset the country when the word of Potbelly's death is made public, we might be able to spring our compatriots. There will be three, possibly four, different factions wanting to move into the vacated throne of the dictator. It will be an ideal time to save our friends. With four different battles going on inside the government for control and with all the distractions, the countrywide movement started by Sunny can take advantage of the situation and move in. One of the factions who will be wrestling for control has given Sunny a wink and a nod. If they succeed, we'll throw in with them.

"Mary Soso will meet with David, and when she reports back, we'll know what our next move will be."

The guards were too gentle with the four Westerners, which led to the suspicion that they were going to put them on display in a televised murder trial. It would be the objective of the Potbelly government to embarrass the free governments of the West.

Quint paced the huge cell they'd been placed in and noted, "I believe we're in for some serious shit here. They evidently didn't catch or sink the trawler, so we have become the single object of their undivided attention. There is no way for us to prove we didn't take down the dictator and no way for them to prove we did. But since we were in their waters illegally and they control the fucked-up corrupt court system, we have no legs."

Jake was standing next to the cell door when an official-looking guard walked up and stood there looking at the four of them. He kept looking around, as if someone was going to join him.

Finally, he spoke in broken English. "Hello. My name is David Soso, and I may be able to help you escape from this place. Tomorrow there will be great turmoil in the country when the announcement of our leader's assassination is announced. Sunny's people may be in a position to make an attempt to take control of the government. While the attention is elsewhere, we can get you out of here. Kim has a plan." He didn't get to finish. Another guard came down the hallway yelling for him. He lowered his voice. "I must report to the warden. Stand by. Be ready to move at any moment."

He turned and yelled something to the other guard and followed him.

Ingrid, who had been in lots of Soviet-style prisons, thought there was no such thing as an easy escape. "We don't know this guy from sour apples. He may be setting us up for an escape attempt, so they can claim we tried and they had to shoot us. Who knows who will be in charge of the government by this time tomorrow?"

Quint nodded in agreement. "We need more than this guy's word before we make a break for it and get dumped on by a firing squad."

Sue responded, "When he comes back, we'll have to give him some kind of test."

David returned shortly. "The idiot warden wanted to move you to a more secure detention center. I tried to explain to him that the change of leadership may not be in his favor, and he'd be putting himself in a bad light if the wrong people take charge. I convinced him to leave things as is until the dust settles."

Quint was trying to come up with a question to convince them that this guy was for real. He asked, "How well do you know Kim?"

"I don't know him at all. I just relayed information to him about the situation here and what we could do about it. Why do you ask?"

"How well to do you know Sunny?"

David looked puzzled. "What are you getting at?"

Quint gave up trying to be clever. "We don't know you from Adam. How do we know you can be trusted?"

David had a look of relief on his face as he answered, "Damn! I thought you thought I was clearly the enemy. I can assure you, I sat with Sunny many evenings talking of freedom for our country, and he told me stories of your last visit here. The escape by sea was remarkable."

"Okay, David, that clears up any doubts we had about you. We are strangers here, and being careful has kept us alive so far. So where are we with getting the hell out of here?"

"I'm meeting with Kim in the morning. I'll lay out the schedule of the prison, and we'll pick a time to make our move. The biggest problem is where we go after the escape is accomplished. The country will be in a complete lockdown, so moving about will be very risky."

Sue, who had been uncharacteristically quiet up to this point, said, "Is there a way to get Kim in here?"

David almost jumped out of his uniform. "What you're asking is akin to suicide. We're trying to get people out, not in. His picture is in every police station in the country. What good could come of bringing him here? Next to Sunny, he's the most wanted man on the planet."

"What if you tell the warden that you have information on the whereabouts of Kim and point out that if you were allowed to capture him, he'd have a leg up with the new administration, whoever that will be?

He would have four Westerners who killed their leader and a notorious guerilla in his prison.

"Once you get permission to capture Kim, you take as many guards as he'll let you and go to the compound. Kim will allow you in. Then you ask the guards if they want to be part of the revolution. Those who do will join the team in the compound. The others will be taken prisoner. You exchange uniforms with the new prisoners, and take the group along with Kim back to the prison. You'll have enough firepower to take over, release all the inmates for additional help, and be sure the warden dies in the attack. If a friendly takeover of the government doesn't take place, you can stay on at the prison and blame the attack and escape on the incompetent leadership of the warden. You'll be recognized for your selfless attention to duty for the communist state. When the smoke clears, you'll be in a position to help the guerillas from the inside as you do now."

Quint remarked, "Damn that was a mouthful. It sounds good to me. What do you think, Jake? Ingrid?"

Both nodded in agreement, and Ingrid added, "This will work, and if the good guys win the struggle for control–all the better. But where the hell do we go once we're outside the walls?"

Sue retorted, "That'll be up to Kim and David."

David looked a little overwhelmed by the suggestion he take over the prison, but after a short pause, he said, "I'll get with Kim and work this out. It might work because of the confusion on the outside." He turned and limped back down the hall. He had a hitch in his getalong.

Quint said, "I think you scared the shit out of David. He's not used to being in the crosshairs. Gathering and disseminating information is a lot different than putting your life in the line of fire. I think Kim will have to help him over the hump of his doubts."

Jake had listened quietly to the banter, and now he put his two cents in. "You, know, we're in the middle of one explosive situation. There isn't a faction in this country that is stable, except for the guerillas. They are focused; they know what their goals are and how to get there. But for the rest, they are as unpredictable as the weather. We don't have a clue how they will react.

"The situation is going to be one big-ass snafu. When we get out of here, it might be prudent to lie low somewhere—wait for the storm to blow over and see who sits on the throne. The compound sounds good to me. We know where it is and what's there, and if we have to, there is enough firepower to defend it."

Sue rejected that notion. "I think we need to get out of the country as soon as possible. We're not popular, as you know, and our round eyes will not be favored, no matter who takes the reins. The new leaders will try to play the imperialist card and execute us. Let's boogie on out of here."

Ingrid threw in with Sue. "From my experience, hanging around in a country after being in prison is not a good thing. Once you escape, you are marked for good, especially if your skin and features are different from the masses. We'll stand out like a giraffe in a wading pool. After we escape, our goal should be to find our way to the closest border."

They had to can the chatter as two guards came by on their regular schedule, checking to be sure the Westerners hadn't disappeared. The guards gave them ugly looks and rattled the bars with their nightsticks, trying to prod the group into giving them an excuse to open the door and give them a lesson in manners towards their masters.

Quint smiled at the guards, giving them a thumbs up, half wishing they'd open the cell, so they could start the escape early.

After the guards had passed, Ingrid bent over in the corner, pulled her pants down, removed the pistol she'd put in her crotch area, and threw it to Quint.

"Damn, Ingrid, how did you manage that?"

"One has to be inventive when one is a prisoner of the communists, as we're finding out."

"Thanks, Wonder Woman! This might help us get the ball rolling when the time is right."

Sue shrugged her shoulders. "I ditched mine. It was a lot bigger than Ingrid's."

"Kim, I've had a vision. I saw Sunny last night as I was cleaning the backroom of the office. I was looking out the rear window and saw him float by. He smiled at me. God has answered my prayers."

Mary Soso stood in front of Kim with her head bowed, only looking up when she mentioned Sunny's name. She positively glowed in the dark, expressing her gratitude for the return of Sunny from the depths of the sea. "He will lead us to victory."

Kim looked down at Mary with all the admiration one could give another, knowing she would step in front of a train if it somehow helped the people attain their freedom from the communists. He thought, *If I had an army of Marys, this battle would be short-lived.*

"Mary, I have good news for you. Your sighting was indeed correct. Sunny has returned from the sea. He'll be speaking to the whole compound tonight, and you'll be sitting next to him when he does. He told me he felt your presence when he was thrown overboard during he storm. Your spirit guided him to safety."

Mary looked up one more time with tears in her eyes, turned, and in her measured steps, returned to her duties.

Kim pulled his soft side together and walked over to Sunny's quarters. He was eager for the details of Sunny's survival, of how Sunny had defied death for the umpteenth time. The story had to be a whopper, considering the conditions the night he was washed overboard into the huge swells that swamped his boat.

He knocked at the door to Sunny's room and let himself in. Sunny looked much restored after a shower, a change of clothes, and a good night's sleep.

"Okay, Sunny, what the hell happened?"

Sunny's expression was that of a college professor teaching a class of freshmen. "I can't tell you how close I was to death's door. When Ingrid slipped from my grasp, the wave washed me over the side and into a huge swell that took me to the peak, dumping me into another swell. That went on for God knows how long.

"When the seas calmed for a bit, I gathered myself and took a quick inventory of what was on my person. I assure you there wasn't much. The life jacket saved me for sure, as well as having a waterproof flashlight. There were lights of a navy ship near where we lost the boat, but I couldn't see anything as small as people in the water. It didn't figure the others had any better chance for survival than I did, other than the fact they were closer to the navy ship. And even if they were rescued, would that really be a good thing? At the time I was busy trying to figure out a way to beat the high seas.

"There were more lights from the navy ships, but none came anywhere near me, and after an hour, they figured I'd bought the farm, as the Americans say. The water was icy cold, and I knew my body would be stiff in another few minutes.

"With the last of my strength I prayed for the salvation of my country and prepared to accept my fate. I started swimming farther out to sea. The thought of those commie bastards finding my body and using it in some propaganda film didn't appeal to me. When I was exhausted to the point of sinking more than swimming, a hand grabbed me.

"I could hear voices speaking a tongue that I was familiar with but couldn't understand. I was barely conscious and couldn't put two and two together."

"I'll be damned!" Captain Bagmanovich exclaimed as they pulled Sunny into the small lifeboat. "This is our friend Sunny. Jesus, he looks dead! Strip his clothes off and put some warm blankets over him."

The small lifeboat with the captain and two crew members was all that the navy destroyer had left after the short, one-sided naval battle. The trawler had taken a couple of direct hits and had no way to return fire, so the captain had put the trawler on course for a head-on collision with the bigger ship as they let go the lifeboat and abandoned ship.

The trawler hit the destroyer at midships, making a small dark spot where it exploded and sank. It was so dark, the navy couldn't see the lifeboat. Thinking the trawler had committed suicide, they didn't search any further for survivors.

Captain Bagmanovich asked his two shipmates, "Is he still alive?" They nodded as they rubbed Sunny's body down, trying to get the circulation going again.

Before long, Sunny began to show signs of life. The captain said, "Don't get excited, Sunny, we're not out of the woods yet. If the sea doesn't get us, come daylight we might be spotted by aircraft or a ship."

It was nearly daylight when the men in the small lifeboat, using Sunny's flashlight, signaled a ship in the distance, not caring if it was the enemy or not. They were freezing and wouldn't last much longer in the cold, turbulent water. The flashlight batteries were nearly exhausted when the ship sent them a signal and headed their way. The captain said a little prayer to the gods of the sea that it be a friendly ship.

As the ship came alongside, it was a joy to see the Russian flag on the mast. Captain Bagmanovich had called for assistance before they abandoned ship, knowing there were other Russian trawlers in the area working for Mr. Wing.

"We're in luck, Sunny! The captain of this vessel is an old friend. He'll take us ashore. You can get back to your revolution, and I can see about another ship. With all the confusion that'll be taking place after the word is out about the dictator, it might be easy to get ashore. No one will know who's in charge."

"So the trawler delivered me back to shore and here I am," Sunny explained. "The captain boarded the trawler, heading for China and looking for another command. So fill me in on what's going on from this end."

Kim explained the situation in the country and the prison. "I think it's an opportunity that won't come along again in our lifetime. We should strike with what we have."

"Not so fast, Kim. Let's think this through. Are you talking about the prison break or the opportunity to make a difference in who leads the country after the dust clears?"

"Both."

"Okay. When do we take over the prison?"

"David will ask permission to take the guards needed to capture me when he arrives for his regular night shift. The warden will grant David's request, hoping to make a big hit with the government heads when he captures the notorious Kim.

"David and his guards will make the trip to the compound here and then return to take down the prison. Of course, you and I will be along to help. We have to be sure the warden dies so that David can assume command."

Sunny asked, "Then what? You have the prison, the prisoners are free, and we have four Westerners to get out of the country. When the four would-be power brokers begin to show their muscle, the first thing they'll do is close off the borders. They won't want any outsiders giving one or the other assistance.

"I have it from a good source that if a certain faction wins the struggle, they'll be friendly to our cause. They will notify me if our help is needed. They won't put us in jeopardy if they don't see a good chance for success. But regardless of what is going on now in the capital, we need to save our friends who made the whole convoluted mess possible."

Kim nodded in agreement and suggested it was about time for Sunny to address the compound. He stepped out of Sunny's room and shouted to a couple of people nearby to gather everyone in front of the main building.

"Listen up!" Kim shouted, standing on the steps above the crowd. "Our leader has risen once again; his nine lives are not yet used up."

The assembled troops showed their approval by clapping and shouting, "Sunny, Sunny."

When Sunny appeared on the steps overlooking the open area of the compound, the troops grew quiet, wanting to hear their leader say the words that would finally allow them to take the offensive in their struggle for freedom.

Standing before his faithful, Sunny said, "Before I say a few words, please make way for Mary Soso to come up to the front. She is the inspiration for our efforts. The symbol of all we stand for."

Mary Soso made her way through the crowd, her steps measured and deliberate and her head bowed in the humility she felt at being singled out. As she approached Sunny, the saintly old woman bowed, clasped her hands, and stopped to pray for their victory. A slight glow seemed to envelope her as she fell to her knees.

Sunny helped Mary to her feet after her short prayer, and she moved behind him, still not looking up. Sunny had trouble speaking, for he was in awe of her presence, as were the rest of the troops.

Finally, with a little cough, he cleared his throat, rubbed his eyes, and began. "We have just witnessed one of the reasons for our struggle. The godless communists have not taken our spirit away. They have only suppressed it for over fifty years. Mary Soso has brought that spirit to light.

"The struggle over the years will show its teeth tonight. We will take advantage of the opportunity presented to us by the death of the dictator. The sea took him and released me.

"Our fight for justice, freedom from tyranny, and the right to practice our beliefs will begin in earnest tonight. We will clean our house, sweeping out the dirt of the past decades.

"I will give the word before dawn where our service will be needed. Get your weapons ready, your minds on the business at hand, and be assured, we will win."

Mary Soso stepped out from behind Sunny, kneeled in front of him, and bowed her head in prayer. Sunny turned and retreated into the office, allowing the saintly old woman to bless the troops.

After a few moments, Kim helped Mary to her feet, and she walked back through the crowded compound to her place at the rear of the assembly as Kim shouted, "Prepare to mount up. Stand by for orders."

David stood in the doorway of the warden's office, his sidearm pointed directly at the warden. He said, "I've come to take over the prison, and you are now my prisoner."

The warden moved quickly to his right, pulling a pistol out of his waistband. He dove behind the couch next to his desk, shooting as he hit the floor. The first round hit David in the right thigh, dropping him to his knees; the other rounds harmlessly sprayed the ceiling.

Hearing the gunfire, Sunny and Kim crashed into the room. David pointed to the couch, and Kim emptied a magazine from his AK-47, hitting the couch from end to end. Sunny followed suit, further destroying the couch.

When no return fire came from the warden, Kim helped David out of the room while Sunny checked behind the sofa. The warden was dead, stitched with bullet holes from head to toe.

Yelling back to the others, Sunny said, "The warden is dead. David, if you're able, get on the intercom system and announce that the prison is now under your command. Ask all the senior guards to come to the office for special orders. We can take away the prison's leadership in one fell swoop; the others will think twice about fighting it out."

The team in their cells below, along with the two guards at the end of the hallway, could hear the gunfire coming from above.

Quint chambered a round in Ingrid's pistol, hoping he wouldn't have to shoot it out with the two guards, who came running down the hallway in a panic with no idea what to do.

When they were close enough to reach, Quint shot the one in front between the eyes, and as he fell forward, Jake reached through the bars and snatched his rifle before it hit the deck. The other guard hesitated long enough for Jake to fire a short burst, killing him instantly. The keys to the cell door were lying on the deck next to the first guard. Sue reached out and grabbed them as Ingrid scooped up the other guard's rifle. With the keys in hand, Sue opened the cell door.

Quint calmly searched the guards for more weapons and their handheld radios. Taking anything they could use, the four escapees headed up the hallway towards the gunfire, hoping the good guys were winning.

David tried the intercom, but it had been sabotaged. "There must be an alert guard here, one who isn't on our side. I think we might have a group loyal to the dictator on the loose. So much for the quick takeover."

"I hear gunfire from below, where the majority of the cells are located," Kim said. You don't suppose Quint has come under fire? Jesus! They're still locked up and defenseless. We better get down there before some idiot decides to execute them during the melee."

They left David to man the communications in the office, took his guards, and headed for the cell area below. As they ran towards the stairs, gunfire ripped the walls and ceiling. They dropped to the deck, thanking their stars the shooter was a lousy shot.

Sunny crawled to the edge of the stairwell. He wanted to throw a hand grenade, but he didn't know where the good guys were. Reaching the edge of the stairwell where it met the wall, he could see a shooter standing in a doorway the next floor down, waiting for them. Sunny jumped up, quickly firing a burst as he rolled down the stairs. The man in the doorway reacted too late. He was hit across the chest and dropped to the floor, dead to the world.

Kim followed Sunny down the stairs as more gunfire sounded from below, sending them an urgent message to hurry.

Again they received fire from a doorway, sending them to the deck. The guards loyal to the dictator were using delaying tactics to keep them from reaching the cells below.

Sunny grabbed the radio he'd taken from the warden's office and called David. "What floor are the cells on where Quint is locked up?"

There was a buzzing and crackling before the voice of Quint came through like he was standing next to Sunny. "Took you guys long enough. We have taken the initiative with a pistol Ingrid had hidden. The two guards who were assigned to us are dead; we have their weapons. We're three floors down. We can hear your gunfire. The bad guys are keeping us pinned down."

The radio suddenly went dead on Quint's end. The transmission was interrupted by David saying, "The capital just called, telling us to kill the Westerners. The dictator's people are still in charge, but I could hear gunfire and explosions in the background, so the issue is in doubt."

Quint came back on. "Son of a bitch shot the radio out of my hand. I had to get the other one. Don't waste any time getting your ass down here. We are just outside the cell where we were being held. Don't get caught up in the battle and forget we have the guards in the middle."

Sunny smiled and said, "Kim, Quint and his team are armed and defending themselves. He said they're pinned down three floors below us. Let's get our asses down there. We know where they are, so now we can push ahead with more force."

Kim took Sunny's advice and threw a hand grenade into the hallway where the automatic fire was coming from. The explosion threw the shooter out of the doorway and into the hall. His body kept others from making their way towards the cells below, giving Kim and the team an opportunity to rush the dictator's faithful stooges. The bad guys were caught in rooms on either side of the hall. Kim took the room on the left,

Sunny the right. It was a short gunfight. The guards had nowhere to run and threw their weapons down. Sunny called David to send a couple of his men to watch the captives.

When David's men arrived, Kim and Sunny continued down the hall, stopping at the head of the staircase just in time to hit the deck and avoid another onslaught of gunfire from the faithful guards, who were in a no-win situation: Quint and his team were blocking them from retreating, and Kim and Sunny were stopping them from moving forward.

Quint yelled into the radio again, "We'll spray the guards from this end while you block them from yours. You'll be shooting down, and we'll be shooting level, so we won't be receiving each other's fire. We're going to move ahead now and let loose with some heavy stuff to distract them."

There was no answer from the radio, but Quint could hear the sound of horrific gunfire.

Sunny and Kim had fired everything they had. The guards didn't have a chance, but they had decided to shoot it out anyway.

The gunfire from Quint's team was devastating. The guards fell back and ran into Kim and Sunny's barrage. The end didn't come soon enough. Stray bullets and shrapnel had hit Sue and Ingrid, causing them both to go down. Two bullets pierced Sue's left shoulder and right hand, while Ingrid was hit by shrapnel in the legs. The guards were all killed in the crossfire, leaving a stack of bodies in the hallway.

Quint looked over in time to catch Sue as she fell from the impact of the bullets. He eased her to the deck and covered her until the shooting stopped.

"Jesus, Sue, what the hell were you thinking? This is getting to be a habit. Covering your ass in this kind of situation isn't nearly as much fun as another I can think of."

"Damn it, Quint. This is no time to be thinking that kind of shit. I'm a hurting unit. Did the bullets go through?"

"Yeah. You're a lucky camper. As you can see, your hand has a nice entrance and exit wound, and the shoulder looks the same. I'll plug the holes so you won't bleed to death."

"That would be nice of you. How is Ingrid? I saw her drop about the same time I did. One of those assholes had to have gotten lucky; they can't shoot for shit."

Ingrid had fallen near Sue, but she couldn't stand up: her legs were full of metal and bleeding profusely.

Sunny and Kim came running down the hall, checking the bodies for wounded who might still have some fight in them. They were all dead.

David called on the radio, "The capital called again, wanting to know if we killed the Westerners. I told them they were dead. The noise in the background sounded the same as before. There is a ferocious battle going on. We still might have a chance to win."

While they were attending to Ingrid, Sunny's cell barked. After a short, one-sided conversation, Sunny closed the cell and called the compound. He told the troops there to stand by. The battle in the capital was still in doubt, and they might be asked to take over the nearby port facilities.

Jake picked the metal out of Ingrid's legs, wrapped them to stop the bleeding, and yelled out to anyone with a radio, "Is there a hospital in this facility?"

Sunny called David and asked if there was a sickbay in the building. David responded, "Yes, just a couple doors down. I have the doctor in here right now tending my wounds and the guards who were hit in the gunfight."

Sunny explained, "We have two good guys down. We'll bring them up as soon as we can stop the bleeding. All the guards are dead. We need to start figuring a way to get Quint and his team out of the country as soon as possible, regardless of how the battle in the capital is going. Win, lose, or draw, we can't take the chance of anyone knowing there was Western influence in the elimination of Potbelly. It has to appear to be an internal affair."

David had been peering out the window of the prison office as he and Sunny spoke, and now in the darkness he could pick out men scurrying in all directions. Taking a closer look, he saw a round being dropped into the tube of a mortar.

"Jesus!" he yelled into the radio. "Sunny, the regular army is out front and they're placing mortars in strategic positions. One is on the way."

The mortar hit short of the roof and scraped the side of the building, hitting the concrete and exploding, but causing no damage.

Sunny asked, "How many do you see? Are we looking at a full-scale attack?"

"I don't know, I can't see the perimeter. I'd say a company force maybe. You know, Sunny, they'll drop as many mortars as they have and not worry about who gets killed, as long as the Westerners die in the attack."

Sunny pondered the situation for a split second and said, "David, hang in there; do the best you can. We'll be up there in a few minutes."

As Sunny spoke, David heard three familiar thumps. The mortars were on the way.

"I have incoming."

The mortars hit, shaking the whole building and sending everyone to their knees.

Sue and Ingrid were huddled in the corner of the cell, ready to move up to the street, but with the new events going on upstairs, Quint told everyone to stay put.

Kim yelled out over the noise, "I'm going up see what the hell is going on. Sunny, you better get your troops up here. He ran to the stairwell and sprinted up the stairs as Sunny got on his cell. His troop leader at the compound answered his cell. "Bring the troops in full combat mode to the prison next to the army headquarters," Sunny ordered. "We have a major battle going here. You are needed ASAP. We are under attack." The next barrage of mortars hit the building's roof, rocking its very foundations.

Kim found David and several of his troops scattered over the office floor. He checked for any signs of life and found none. They all died trying to free their country from the clutches of a fanatical dictator.

Looking around for the doctor, Kim found him in the hospital section working on the wounded, not paying any attention to the carnage going on around him. With a little luck, the next round of mortars wouldn't hit this special place. Kim called Quint and asked him and Jake to arm themselves with rifles and come up to the roof where the mortars had just hit and help him pick off the mortar teams. He figured they wouldn't hit the same target twice, so it would be safe enough to shoot from there.

"Quint, maybe we can hold them off until Sunny's troops get here. Then we'll have another crossfire situation. I'll be on the roof."

Sunny understood the conversation and yelled, "Head up to the roof. "I'll take care of things down here. Go help Kim."

Quint and Jake sprinted up to the roof. When they arrived, Kim hadn't taken a shot yet, not wanting to give their position away until all three could shoot at the same time, knocking out three of the four mortars.

Using the captured rifles of the army troops, they took aim and fired at the same time, hitting their targets. The mortar men still standing were forced to take cover as the three shooters on the roof hit the men manning the fourth mortar at nearly the same time.

Some of the ground troops must have seen the flashes from the roof, as they returned a barrage of automatic weapons fire, forcing the three men to take cover. When Quint peeked over the roof's edge, he saw the mortar men back at their post. But that didn't last long. Sonny's troops had arrived. A volume of fire hit the unsuspecting army troops, killing the entire company.

Quint quickly got on the handheld radio and notified Sunny to bring the wounded up to the prison hospital.

They climbed down from their position and emerged in the front, shaking hands with the troops from the compound.

Kim yelled out orders to secure the perimeter around the prison.

He asked the leader of Sunny's troops, "What have you heard from the capital?"

"The battle is still in doubt."

Sunny met his troop commander in the hospital section. "You came just in time, my friend. I'm sorry to say that David and several of his people died in the second round of mortars. I don't know how to tell Mary Soso that her beloved son has been called to his maker."

The cell vibrated in Sunny's pocket. He listened for a short time and replied, "Very well." Turning off the phone, he announced, "Gentlemen, the port and dock area have been secured by the regular army. The battle in the capital is still raging, and the army here is still loyal to the dictator. I'll take as many troops from here as we can spare and make a fight of it at the docks. Quint, you and Jake need to figure a way to get across the border. Good luck, and thank you for your efforts and support of our cause."

Sunny shook hands with Kim, Quint, Jake, and the wounded warriors, Ingrid and Sue.

"Kim, I know you'd like to come along and be part of the fight, but you've done enough for now, and you'll be more valuable to our cause from afar. Whether we win or lose, a voice is needed on the outside, someone who knows our goals. Thank you."

The last they saw of Sunny, he was waving his troops to follow him into the battle to take on the regular army defending the port.

When Sue and Ingrid had been bandaged and given pain medication, the doctor told them to take it easy for a week or so. Quint had to laugh. "There isn't any R and R on this front. Come on; let's go somewhere a little more private."

The team found an empty office and settled in.

"What we need to do is figure a way to the border," Quint said. "I'm open to suggestions."

"I don't suppose we could book a flight out of the nearest airport or rail station?" Sue remarked.

Jake responded, "Cruise ships don't stop here, the port is in a fierce gun battle, and the only airport is military. So I guess we'll have to become magicians and disappear. Who wants to be first?"

Quint said, "Sue you have just hit a home run."

Sue responded, "We aren't playing baseball, buster. Do you have a point to the home run bullshit?"

"Yes I do, and if you can curb the sarcasm for a moment, I'll explain. I know you're wounded and all, but you haven't lost your sharp tongue. I'm going to let that slide for now.

"If you'll remember your history of the war, there is an item that has gone relatively unnoticed. There are existing railroad tracks running across the border. They've never been torn up. Kim, are you familiar with the train tracks?"

"Yes, I know they exist. I never gave them a thought. You don't hear much about the railroad here. Not enough commerce going on. It's worth a look."

Quint walked over to a map on the wall. "Kim, show me the tracks and the railyard."

After an hour discussing the railyard location and the many ways of getting there, Quint said, "Jake, I'll take Kim, and we'll do a recon on the yard and the best route for us to take the team there if it looks good. You stay and hold down the fort. We can stay in contact with the radios."

Quint and Kim armed themselves with everything they could carry and left to find a ride on the Reading. The battle for the port was in full swing, the flares turning the dock area into daylight. Whose flares they were, they didn't know.

Using his knowledge of stealing cars in his youth, Quint hot-wired the first car they found big enough for five people and headed for the railyard. It wasn't far, according to their map.

"Look! There it is," exclaimed Kim, whose map reading skills had paid off.

Quint parked the car a block away, not wanting any problems with the yard security. It would be better to walk up, and Kim wouldn't be out of place if they were approached.

The security detail had a regular schedule that never varied by a minute. The pair watched them from across the street for two hours. It would be easy to wait for the security car to pass a certain point and then slip into the yard.

The engines were kept inside a huge warehouse structure, the boxcars and rail gang cars in the open yard.

After the security vehicle had passed the third time, Kim and Quint ran into the yard, taking a route that provided the darkest path to the huge doors. At the corner of the building they discovered a small unlocked door that gave them easy access.

Inside were five black engines. They appeared to have been manufactured in a bygone era. The disappointment was obvious on Quint's face. "Jesus, these motors are ancient. It would take a crew of five to operate the fucking things. Damn!"

"Not so fast, Quint. See that small diesel on the other side? Maybe we can pile on that one and make our way to the border. We could hook up a boxcar to have something between us and the bullets if we run into any bad guys leaving the yard or on the way south."

They walked over to the diesel engine, climbed aboard, and spent an hour figuring out how it worked.

"Piece of cake, Kim. All these diesel engines, big or small, work the same. We fire this baby up, and off we go. We'll wait until tomorrow night and make the trip in the dark. We might just get the hell out of here in one piece."

"Shit!" Kim said. He pushed Quint to the floor of the engine. "There's a couple of guards. I don't think they saw us, but they're heading straight for the engine. Damn. We might have to take them out, but if they don't show up for their report, this place will be crawling with the army."

The two soldiers stood by the engine and chatted, looking up and down the track before boarding. Kim smiled at Quint. He whispered, "These two want to hijack the engine and defect to the south. One's a former engineer." He looked down at the two men, who were still talking, and added, "These guys are brothers."

Quint patted Kim on the shoulder. "How do we approach them without scaring them into some kind of action? They have to be on edge, deserting from the army and stealing a train."

"We'll wait until they climb aboard and subdue them. If we say anything now, they'll shoot first and ask questions later. Just as we'd do. We have to use our surprise advantage to capture them."

"Shit! That's risky as hell. What if they turn out to be a couple of black belt karate experts, and they make mincemeat out of us, if not kill us!"

Kim chuckled at the pale-faced Quint. "Jesus, Quint, you read too many books. When they get up here, we throw down on them, and I'll talk very fast to let them know we're on their side. You might not help much, being a round-eyed, white-skinned infidel.

"Okay, get ready. They're climbing aboard."

Quint and Kim slipped behind the huge electric generators. When the two guards turned their backs to them, they would attack, counting on surprise to subdue the two.

"When I say go, we jump them," whispered Kim.

The guards climbed up to the control room of the engine and began to cut wires and pull plugs. They were disabling the engine, which didn't make sense if they were planning to use it for their escape.

Kim whispered, "Now!" The attack was a complete surprise, but success was not guaranteed.

Quint's guy fell and hit his head on the deck, knocking himself out, but Kim's guy turned around quick enough to send Kim backwards with a round-house karate kick to his midsection.

Kim responded with a little martial arts of his own, only to be kicked again with a right foot to his leg, bringing him to his knees. When the guy was over him, about to throw the death blow, Quint hit him in the back of the head with the other guard's rifle butt.

Kim looked up, surprised to be on his knees, and said, "Thanks, Quint."

"Not a problem, Kim, I read it in a book. It said something like, don't fuck with someone who is meaner than you are!"

The two army guards were out cold on the deck of the engine. They'd have to wait for them to come around and try to convince them they were on the same track, so to speak. They tied the soldiers back to back to keep them from communicating when they came to.

Kim asked, "How did you knock your guy out?"

Quint was tempted to tell a whopper to pay Kim back for his earlier remarks, but just told it as it was. "He tripped on the uneven plating and fell. He knocked himself out."

The two guards began to moan as they came around and turned their heads to see who cold-cocked them. When one began to speak, Kim told him in Zazakuren to zip it up and keep quiet. They would know soon enough what was going on.

He went on to explain that he'd heard them talking about desertion and going south, so they had something in common. "Sorry about the rough handling, but it was the only way to keep from having a gunfight. My friend and I want to head south. Maybe we can plan something for all of us to find our way to freedom. There are three more, and we need to be out of the country ASAP. We thought of stealing an engine and one boxcar, taking our chances on the rails. But why were you sabotaging this engine?"

They didn't speak for a few moments. Then one spoke up. "We didn't want this engine to move. It's very fast and could catch anything on the tracks. We'd planned to stow away on a freight train. When it arrived at the border, we would capture the engine and keep going, busting through the fence."

Kim quickly translated for Quint, and then responded, "Sounds good to us. Would you like some company on your journey?"

The one with the bump on the back of his head asked, "Will you untie us?"

Kim took a long look into the eyes of the one who made the request, and said, "Yes."

"Quint, keep your gun on these two, until we make a deal. I think they're sincere. It appears they are twins, now that I look at them. You know what they say—they all look alike."

Quint responded, "How do you come up with all the bullshit? This is a dead-ass serious situation, and you're making ethnic slurs. Jesus, Kim, get serious!"

"That's your problem, Quint—Mr. Serious all the time. Lighten up."

When the twins were released, they grew more friendly, and Kim discovered they were from a village near where he grew up. The bonds of friendship began to flower.

The twins told Kim of their plan to escape as stowaways on the regular freight run from the port city to the southern border. It would be easy with all the turmoil in the country since the death of the dictator.

Kim couldn't tell the two apart, so he asked one of them to remove his hat.

Quint told Kim, "Ask them again why they're taking this engine apart. Their first answer was under duress."

Kim pointed to the one without the cover. "Why were you sabotaging this motor?"

The hatless one responded, "We are creating all the confusion we can. This is the third one we've worked on, and as I said before, it's the fastest."

Kim pressed them for their plan to stow away on the regular run south. "Okay, so how do you plan to get on the train without being noticed and then take over the engine just north of the border?"

The one still wearing his hat said, "I'm the oldest. When you have a question, I'll do the talking. Once every two weeks there is a work call at the railroad station. All those who want to go to the border and do hard labor for the army will be loaded into a couple of box cars. The work usually lasts a couple of weeks. When the new workers arrive, the others who have been there for two weeks come back. Because the work is hard and dirty, with little pay, it's difficult to fill the jobs. They're not picky about who goes."

Kim pondered what the hat had said and asked, "They don't ask for papers?"

"No. You just line up and file into the box cars. We've waited a long time for the right opportunity to escape. Our parents were killed in a riot a year ago, so we don't have anyone left for the government to hold over us. But it won't be easy getting a round-eye on the train. Are there more Westerners?"

"Yes, three more. Two of them are women. Both are wounded from the battle at the prison. I suppose you heard about that?"

"My brother and I were supposed to go there with our company, but we deserted early. We were going to hide out here until morning. We'll put on some civilian clothes and board the train.

"With the government under attack, they fear the borders may be breached, so they're taking more people south to beef up the construction of defensive positions."

Kim translated the last to Quint, who looked at the twins and said, "Good thing you didn't go with your company. They were completely wiped out trying to take control of the prison."

When Kim translated, the twins gave their first visible show of concern. Until that moment they'd been stoic—no facial expressions of any kind to reveal their thoughts.

The hat said sadly, "We had close friends in the company who wanted to defect too, but leaving family would have meant the death penalty for those left behind. You're sure they were all killed?"

"Yes. I'm sorry to hear someone died who wanted to defect and gain their freedom."

Kim was going to ask the twins their names, but decided against it. It would be better they didn't know in case they were captured. It was good that the two be known only as Hat and No Hat.

Quint was getting an itchy feeling and remarked to Kim, "I have a skin-crawling feeling. It's time to go back to the prison and get the gang ready for a train ride. We need to figure a way to disguise our pale faces and round eyes."

"Yes," said Kim, and I'm a lead-pipe cinch to be caught if I speak to anyone. I've acquired a Western accent from my years in Canada."

"You can pretend that you're deaf and dumb, while we become lepers or something to keep people away."

Kim replied, "That might be a good idea—wearing old rags while I clear the way for you. No one will want to be near you. I can understand the feeling."

He smiled, and they bid their new friends goodbye until the following morning at the station dock where the volunteer workers lined up.

Chapter Eleven

The Train

Quint fired up the stolen car, and they headed back to the prison, staying away from the battle at the docks.

When they pulled up to the prison, everyone was barricaded near the front entrance. Jake waved for them to pull the car into the side street facing the port.

As they parked the car, there was an explosion inside the prison, blowing what was left of the windows out. Glass flew into the side street, hitting the car as they instinctively ducked inside it.

"Jesus. I thought we cleared the prison," yelled Quint as they ran to the protection of the barricade, sliding behind a wall of sandbags.

Jake, who was firing his rifle at the windows and roof, said, "Somehow we missed a squad or so of loyal troops. They have been giving us fits since you left. Their leader yelled for us to surrender to them. I had to laugh. He won't come out of the building to attack us. He's just using his grenades and automatic fire to harass us. If he makes a small mistake, I'll nail him."

Quint said, "You keep him busy, while we get Sue and Ingrid into the car. Then we'll pick you up. We can spend what's left of the night at the railroad yard.

We've figured a way to get to the border. Our train will leave early in the morning. All we need is some rags to wear. I'll explain later."

Jake responded, "Okay, let's get to it. Better yet, why don't you and I go inside and take these fuckers out? Kim can put the girls in the car. We don't need these sorry-ass excuses for soldiers following us."

"Okay. I'm game."

Kim, who was standing next to Jake, heard his brilliant idea and said, "Wait a minute. What makes you think you're the qualified dynamic duo? I don't have a say in this plan?"

Quint retorted, "No, you don't. If something happens to us, you're the only one who can get Sue and Ingrid across town and into the station. If you go down, we don't have an expert in the native language to cover our asses, even though you speak with a foreign accent and hardly look native. You could even pass for a Wall Street broker. But you're all we got. So get them to the car and come back for us. We won't be long."

They disappeared into the building in a flash, with bullets hitting all around them from the second-story windows.

Kim and Ingrid sprayed the floor hoping to keep the shooters down or even hit someone.

When Jake and Quint rolled through the doorway, a hail of bullets met them, spitting shrapnel in all directions. Two shooters were at the head of the stairwell shooting down on them.

Quint's position gave him an opportunity to cover Jake as he dove across the aisle to the hallway, taking himself out of sight of the shooters. He emptied his magazine at the two, but only managed to make them duck out of the line of fire. He yelled over at Jake after he had reached the protection of the wall, "Damn! This might not have been such a hot idea."

"No shit, Quint. What do you suggest now, since your first suggestion really sucks? This may take awhile."

"I'm going to crawl around to the foot of the stairs, and while you keep their heads down, I'll make my way up the stairs."

"Ten-four, go when you're ready."

Quint crawled to the corner of the hallway, and when Jake started firing at the head of the stairs, he sprinted up. When he reached the landing, the bullets were passing over his head. He dove for the first doorway. As he rolled in, one of the shooters was so surprised he missed with a short burst, giving Quint the opportunity to take him out with a well-placed round from his Colt .45.

After he dropped the guy, Quint tossed a grenade down the hall as he did a swan dive into the next room. When the grenade exploded, he yelled down to Jake,

"Come on up the stairs. I've cleared the hallway. Take the first room on the right."

When Jake yelled he'd made it up the stairs, Quint let loose another grenade and moved to the next room. He found two dead in the hallway. The second room had one dead with his rifle still warm from firing.

While he was checking the body out, Jake slipped into the room. "Well, I suppose you have a good idea where the rest of the squad is?"

"Hell, I don't know. We just keep working our way down the hall, and when we've killed ten or so, that's probably all there is. I think there are more weapons lying around than there are bodies to man them. I believe some may have deserted. I'm sure they know the whole country is in turmoil and found this a perfect opportunity to hit the road running. Why die for a dictator's last grip on the country?"

"Let's go. I'll check the rooms on the right, and you go left. We're about out of hand grenades, so we'll have to do it the hard way until we reach the warden's office. I think that's where they'll make their stand."

"I have a better idea: let's set the building on fire. I'm surprised it hasn't burned up already. We set fires in all the rooms back towards the stairs and then get the fuck out. We'll save some time, some weapons, and our own asses."

Using the kerosene from a space heater, Quint wet the desk and chairs in the room.

Lighting the kerosene, they moved to the next room and the next, until that end of the building was aflame. Just for good measure, they stacked their remaining grenades in a bucket placed in the middle of the entranceway. Jake set one grenade on the top of the pile, so they could shoot it and set the bucketful off, blowing the entrance to the building into rubble.

When they got to the street the second floor was blazing, and there was no shooting from the windows.

Sue held the door open as they piled into the car. Jake remarked, "I think any pukes we didn't kill deserted." The words hadn't left Jake's lips before the car was hit by a hail of gunfire. Lucky for them, no one was hit.

"Jesus, Jake, will you stop making predictions? Every time you come up with some words of wisdom, the shit hits the fan. Come on, Kim, put the hammer down." Quint's words didn't fall on deaf ears. The four-door car careened down the street, dodging the debris scattered in every direction.

It was nearly eight hours since the first shot had been fired, and it seemed like a short dream. Shortly before dawn the car pulled into the railroad station's huge and nearly empty parking area.

Kim drove the car past the lot into the railyard's side tracks, where the empty boxcars were stored. He stopped at an empty car to let Ingrid, Sue, and Jake out to take refuge and set up a safe environment for the short layover until they boarded the train south.

Kim and Quint took the car back to the parking lot to keep it handy in case Murphy rained on their parade.

As they walked back to the boxcar, the predawn light let them see what a mess the railyard was. It appeared that most of the cars hadn't been moved in years. The only track that wasn't rusted over was the main track running north and south and a few side tracks for changing out cars and engines.

According to the twins, there was a roundhouse at the border, where the engine was used to push, rather than pull on the way back north. That's where they would jump ship, so to speak.

Quint said, "I'll go check out the staging-area dock for the workers. I'll meet you back at the boxcar."

Kim put up a hand to stop him. "Don't you think I should do that? You hardly look like a native seeking work. You'll stick out like a coyote in a sheep's pen."

"You have a point, Kim. You take care of the recon, and I'll go get the troops ready for the short walk to the loading dock. We'll have to find some rags to put on. The engine repair shop would be a good place to find those, I suspect. See you in a while."

Quint located the repair shop on his way back to the boxcar. He heard the sound of voices and laughter inside. Using his ghostly skills to approach anything he thought could be dangerous, he made his way inside without a sound.

Slipping behind a workbench, he could see people juggling, throwing knives, and tumbling. It seemed there was a circus in town. The troupe looked to be European, and their language sounded like Russian. Quint retreated from the shop and hurried back to the boxcar.

"Ingrid, do you feel well enough to take a walk? There's a Russian circus troupe in the repair shop. We need to find out what their status is. They could be our ticket out of here," Quint said excitedly.

Ingrid stood, wincing from pain. "Yes, but I'll need some assistance if it's very far. My legs are really hurting. If they are Russian, I can find out what they're doing here and for how long. I imagine with the civil war in progress, they want to get out as much as we do."

"Jake, you come and help me with Ingrid. Sue, you hold down the fort." Quint's voice had settled down a little, but still betrayed his excitement at the possibility of falling in with the Russians.

The sun was breaking over the turbulent city, with the smoke of battle giving the coming light an eerie glow. It looked more like a sunset than a sunrise.

They made good time back to the shop, despite Quint's having to carry Ingrid most of the way. The repair shop had a door big enough to allow a train engine inside and a smaller door to admit people. Ingrid knocked on the smaller door.

Not a sound came from within, so Ingrid knocked again and rattled something off in her native language.

"What did you say, Ingrid?" asked Quint.

"I asked someone to come and open the door. I suppose they counted heads, and no one was missing, so they're suspicious, and with good cause."

The door opened ever so slowly, and a young woman peeked out. "I'm Russian," Ingrid said. "Help me, please. My legs are hurting from the gunfire in the city."

The woman called out and shut the door.

"What did she say, Ingrid?" Jake asked.

"She asked their leader to come to the door."

The door opened enough for a voice to be heard. "Who are you, and what do you want?" asked a female voice.

Ingrid was losing patience. "Open the fucking door, for Christ's sake. I'm in pain and need help. Do I look like the KGB?" The door opened all the way.

The speaker announced that she was the leader of the circus gang.

Ingrid asked if she could come inside, and the leader nodded. Ingrid pushed her way through the door, followed by Quint.

"Who is the real leader of this troupe? I have important questions for him."

The woman repeated. "I'm the leader."

Ingrid asked, "Would you please tell me if you're getting out of the country anytime soon?"

"Yes, tomorrow morning. We have it on good authority that a train will leave early for the border. We don't want to get involved in the hostilities here. We want to go home. We've been given permission to take the supply train south and out of the country."

"Four of my friends and I have found ourselves in a bad predicament," said Ingrid. "We need to get out of the country. It would be better if I don't go into detail about our circumstances, but be assured our situation is desperate. Does your permit have a specific number of people allowed to leave?"

"No, but we have a guide with us. He's not here right now, but he will be here to lead us to the staging dock and put us on the train for the trip south. He's responsible for our safe departure, because the dictator doesn't want to piss off our government."

Ingrid asked, "Do you know about the demise of the dictator and the battle in the capital city for control of the country?"

"My gosh! No! We didn't know about the seriousness of the situation. The guide has kept us in here without any outside communication. We did hear the explosions and gunfire, but didn't know the why of it, not wanting to get involved and put our departure in jeopardy. Will the fighting affect the train schedule, and what is your situation?"

"We were involved somewhat in the elimination of the brutal dictator and were taken prisoner. There was a battle at the prison, giving us a chance to escape. I was wounded in the fight. Would you consider adding us to your troupe? We could blend in and be out of your hair once we cross the border."

The leader of the group was clearly in a quandary, wanting to help her countryman, but in turn not wanting to put her troupe in danger.

"How would we add you to the group and not be noticed by our guide?"

"Our group includes a man born in this country; his name is Kim. He could replace your guide."

"You know, Ingrid, we aren't in favor of dictators or suppressive governments, but I can't put my people in danger for your safety. We'd have to kill the guide or at least disable him for the time it takes to get out of the country. You're asking a lot."

Ingrid continued, "This country is at a crossroads in its history. Tomorrow the government could be one for freedom, or the loyalists of the dictator could keep the throne. Our lives and yours will be in danger if the dictator's people stay in control. We promise not to kill the guide, and once we're on the train to disassociate ourselves from you. All we need is the opportunity to get on the train." The leader considered this and then responded, "I'll have to present your request to the whole crew. If they agree to take you on, then we will."

Quint and Ingrid stepped outside the shop and watched the sun coming up, hoping their next sunrise would be in the country to the south.

Shortly, the Russian leader came to the door and asked them to come back in. "We have decided to help you, but only to board the train. After that you'll be on your own. We'd like to meet Kim."

Ingrid translated, and Quint replied, "Tell her I'll go get the rest of the group."

Quint hurried back to the boxcar, gathered everyone around, explained the turn of events, and added, "Kim, you're going to be a communist guide for our escape. We have a golden opportunity to take our leave from this convoluted mess. Let's go."

Kim, not too cool with the idea of being a communist, asked, "Why do I have to be the communist? I'm trying to get away from these scumbags, not be one. I think you guys are picking on me because we don't look alike."

"No shit, Kim. You are the man today because you don't look like us. Now let's get our asses over there before the guy whose job you're going to take over arrives."

Without any further discussion they made their way over to the repair shop and found Ingrid and the Russian circus troupe in a violent struggle with the communist guide.

Quint and Kim jumped into the fray, while Jake helped Ingrid and Sue to a safe distance. The guide had been a handful for the troupe, they not having experience in the fine art of submission fighting.

It didn't take long for Quint and Kim to subdue the guide, being very careful not to kill him.

"You are similar to the guide," said the troupe leader to Kim. "You shouldn't have any trouble leading us aboard the train. He has all the papers we need in the briefcase, and by the way, it's nearly time to get over there. We should be on our way."

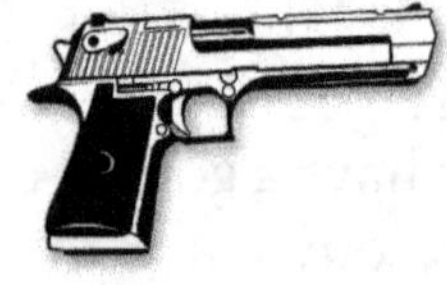

Chapter Twelve

The Journey South

Quint tied the guide up and was in the process of gagging him when he rattled off a string of unintelligible gobbledegook.

Kim smiled and translated the rapid-fire utterings. "He wants us to let him go because he's not loyal to the communists. He was only going along to get along. If we let him go, he'll disappear from us and the government."

Quint questioned, "How do we know he'd not full of shit?"

Kim pondered the question for a minute and suggested, "If we take his identification away, he's up the creek. He'll have a hard time convincing anyone who he is. And even if he does, how will he explain the loss of a whole Russian circus troupe? I'm sure he'd be better off deserting than trying to cover his ass."

Kim told him to sit tight for two hours, and then he could take off. He warned the man that they would have someone watching the shop. If he left early, a bullet would find him.

They left him loosely tied to the workbench, gathered their gear, and headed for the staging dock.

The staging area was a clusterfuck, with a mob waiting to catch the train and get away from the battle, which was no longer confined to the port. The soldiers were having a hard time keeping control.

Kim told the circus people to stand by while he pushed his way through the throng to find the officer in charge.

The officer was standing at the edge of the platform, urging his soldiers to keep the crowd back from the track so the train could pull up and begin loading.

Kim approached the officer, presented his papers, and sought permission to bring the Russians to the front of the line.

The officer looked over the papers. He was clearly not pleased to allow a bunch of foreigners to load first, if at all, but he didn't have a choice. The papers were signed by a general with whom he was familiar. He recognized the general's seal, and without enthusiasm, he told his troops to make a hole and bring the Russians up to the front.

The throng of bodies was pressing forward, the ones in the back wanting to get closer. The soldiers were getting anxious as they were starting to lose control of the situation. The officer waved the train forward, wanting to get the thing loaded and out of his hair.

As the old steam train approached, a surge in the crowd nearly pushed those in front onto the tracks and under the slow-moving train. That caused the guards to fire their weapons in the air, to scare the people into backing off.

When the train stopped, Kim helped Sue and Ingrid aboard the first boxcar, while Jake and Quint kept the crowd from jumping into the car with them.

The angry crowd had reached a fever point when all the noise from the battle in the port area ceased as quickly as it had started, causing the pushing and shoving to stop.

They were all wondering who had won the battle. It didn't take long to find out, as a column of vehicles came roaring across the trainyard. The lead vehicle slammed to a stop near the engine. The other trucks, showing automatic weapons, surrounded the crowd of people. The army officer on the platform didn't have to look twice to see his people had lost the battle, and it was time for him to take a powder. He and the other soldiers disappeared into the crowd, their weapons lying where they had been standing, along with their shirts and military hats.

The leader of the arriving partisans dismounted from the truck, held his weapon up at the engineer, and ordered him to step down.

He said, "We are commandeering this train. You will take us south to the border so we can continue our assault on the communist forces. Tell everyone on the train to dismount and make room for my soldiers and equipment."

The engineer replied, "I have only one boxcar loaded, and it's full with a Russian circus troupe."

The leader of the partisans walked over to the boxcar door. "Who's in charge here?"

Kim stepped forward. "I am. I've been ordered to get these people out of the country so we don't piss off the Russians."

"Is this the lot of you?"

"Yes, we are all here."

"I'll have to check with my leader about this."

Kim asked, "Is your leader Sunny?"

"Yes—how did you know that?"

"We are close friends, and he knows about us. When you talk to him, tell him Kim, Quint, and friends are loaded on the train and would like to continue south out of the country."

The rebel leader walked back to the truck and made a call from the cab. He returned after a few minutes, saluted Kim, and said, "You, my friend, are welcome to take the train as far as you want. Sunny bids you well, and says he'll contact you down the road. He added that the news from the capital is good." He was about to say something else when a bullet hit him between the eyes. He dropped to the tracks, dead to the world.

A sniper's bullet had found him, followed by an attack from some loyalists who had escaped the battle and found their way to the railyard hoping to hijack a train south.

The engineer turned and ran back to the engine, climbed aboard, and began to feed the boilers to get up enough steam to get moving.

Quint, dodging the bullets from the attackers, ran behind the boxcar and unhitched the car behind them, leaving only their car attached to the engine.

The mob of people lay on the ground ducking bullets flying between the rebels and loyalists. As the engine began to move, Kim, Jake, and Quint jumped aboard, sliding the door shut. Bullets bounced off the metal.

As the engine and the boxcar picked up speed, the firing became faint. They were on their way south to the border. "Damn, that was too fucking close," was all Quint could mutter as he slid the boxcar door open. "I'm going to climb up and talk to the engineer. It's a long trip, and there are a few things we need to know up front. Like how many stops does he need to make, will there be soldiers at any of the stops, and does he have communication with them? It's particularly important to know if he has to slow down for any steep grades. That would be the opportune time for anybody on our trail to try and bag us. Kim, are you familiar with this route?"

"No, but I think I'll come with you. Did it occur to you that you don't speak his language?"

"Details, always details. Okay, let's go."

The engine was at full throttle as they climbed out of the rocking boxcar. The old coal-fired steam engine was groaning with the stress of running wide open. Black smoke was filling the air as they careened down the track. Getting to the coal storage bin was actually a rigorous endeavor, because boxcars are not made for a person to go from the siding opening to the end of the car and arrive with relative safety at the ladder waiting to be used.

Quint reached the ladder first and helped Kim, whose big feet didn't fit into the small spaces between the corrugated sides of the car. That and his short stature made it difficult for him to reach the first rung of the ladder.

When they made it to the top of the car, it was not easy to walk to the rear of the old engine. The railroad ties below looked like a picket fence at a hundred miles an hour. Quint reached the coal storage bin first and waved for Kim to follow him as he crawled over the stored coal.

He could see the engineer sitting at the open window with his hand on the throttle and the fireman shoveling coal into the furnace, keeping the one-car train puffing along at maximum speed.

Quint jumped down to the rear of the engine compartment and yelled, "Hello, mates."

The engineer jumped off his seat, reaching for his sidearm, as the fireman tried to hit Quint with his coal shovel.

Kim pushed past Quint and calmed the engineer and fireman down before they had a full scale battle on their hands.

"Damn, Quint. This guy was a nervous wreck at the trainyard, and now you scared the shit out of him. He could have shot and asked questions later."

"I was just trying to be a friendly passenger. How was I to know this guy not only looks like Barney Fife, but he's just as nervous? Ask him to slow the fuck down. I don't think this old engine will do well on sharp curves. Find out when he needs to stop for coal and water or what have you. And is there any place he needs to check in or make a report by radio?"

After a twenty-minute question and answer session with the engineer while the fireman kept feeding the coal, Kim said, "He has to make two stops for coal and water, maybe just one if we slow down, but he doesn't want to do that. There are only a few curves and three places where the grade is steep enough to slow them down. He would rather keep the speed up and take his chances stopping for fuel. He wants to put as much distance as he can between the train and the commie bastards who are surely on our tail."

"Sue, it would be best to keep still so you don't start bleeding again. We can't do squat while the train is moving," Jake said. He didn't like the confines of the boxcar any more than Sue or Ingrid, but the cards had been dealt, and they had to play the hand out. It was unnerving not being able to see anything other than what was visible through the open sliding door.

As the terrain changed from flat to rolling hills, Ingrid said, "This reminds me of the times I was a captive of the former Soviet Union. I rode in many an old wooden boxcar from one prison camp to another. We should appreciate that this car is metal and provides us some protection.

"Thinking back, I thank God the West didn't fold, which forced the East to move into the twentieth century. We are damn lucky to have a train ride south to the border. It would have been a long trip by car or on foot, although I've done both for longer distances, like the trek across Siberia, a nightmare that comes back to me frequently."

Sue sat back in the corner of the car, taking the meaning of Ingrid's words to heart. It could be a whole lot worse.

Kim said, "I'll hang here with the engineer until the next stop. The thoughts of seeing the railroad ties going by so quickly while I try to traverse from the engine to the boxcar makes my stomach flip up and down like a jumping bean. I'd rather be in a gunfight."

"Okay dude, your choice. I'll head back and let them know what's up. Do you think the engineer and fireman are on our side or just going along to keep from getting shot?"

"You know, Quint, I'm not sure on that one. I better take his sidearm until we find out for sure. We'll know when we make the first stop. You might want to be up here then."

220

The short but adventurous climb back to the boxcar didn't come any easier the second time around. Swinging into the open sliding door, Quint landed in the middle of the car as Jake grabbed him. The momentum would have carried him out the opposite door.

After catching Quint, Jake said, "You better keep your day job. Your prospects for work in the Hollywood stunt arena are not favorable. And that's putting it kindly."

Sue echoed Jake's words. "You better listen to Jake. As impaired as I am, I could have done a better landing than that. How did you ever survive in the field for so long?"

Ingrid grinned at the humorous banter, suggesting, "We might want to get as much rest as we can. We've been up for nearly forty-eight hours."

"Good idea, Ingrid. We have a couple of stops to replenish our coal and water. We're not sure which side the train crew is on, and we might have to fight our way through the stops and slowdowns for steep grades," Quint said. He seated himself and promptly nodded out.

Jake looked over at Sue and asked, "How does he do that? Jeez, it's like he flips on a switch and out he goes."

But Sue was already out when Jake asked the question, and Ingrid, who had her legs propped up on a box to minimize the pain, was nearly asleep herself.

Jake looked around for something to lay his head on, but there was nothing suitable. Ingrid, seeing his fruitless search, suggested, "Hey, wanna share my equipment bag?"

Jake took advantage of her generosity, laying his head next to hers. Even under the circumstances, she had the wonderful perfumed smell of a woman, giving him visions better suited for another time.

Quint was awakened by Jake's whispering, "We're coming to our first stop. The train has been slowing down for some time. Maybe you should climb up to the engine and join Kim in case there's a problem. I'll stay and wake up the troops. We'll get our weapons ready and be on alert for anything that comes our way."

"Okay, Jake. I'll call you on the handheld. I wonder why Kim didn't let us know we were coming to a stop?"

Quint slid out the door and up to the engine, finding Kim and the crew members hanging out of the engine, trying to see what was ahead.

"Kim, why didn't you give us a buzz about stopping?"

"The battery in the radio is weak or dead. I couldn't get anything to work. I figured you'd feel the slowing and come up here. Are they ready for action down there?"

"Yes, they're ready. What does the engineer say about the first stop?"

Kim turned away from the engine window long enough to point out the terrain. "It's steep coming into the fuel stop, and it will be steep going out. So it will be slow going—too slow and an uncomfortable situation. He says the small village didn't have soldiers in the past, but that was before all the turmoil. He's not sure what we'll find. He's afraid of the slow going leaving the village."

The train slowed and came to a stop under a spout hanging down from the water tower. The fireman jumped down from the engine and guided the spout over the water intake funnel. While they were taking on water, two men walked up to the engine, waving their arms in a friendly manner.

The engineer reached for his pistol and, realizing he was unarmed, yelled to Kim, " You might want to be ready. I don't know these men approaching us."

Kim and Quint stepped over in front of the engineer to see who their visitors were.

"Jesus!" escaped from Kim's lips. "How the hell did you two get here? We're a couple of hundred miles from the rail station."

Hat and No Hat were standing on the railroad bed smiling. No Hat said, "We need a ride. Our transportation died, and we're afoot. Will you let us tag along?"

Kim responded, "How the hell did you get here?"

No Hat responded, "The mob of people at the rail-yard pushed us away from the tracks. We couldn't get to the train, so we stole a car and headed for a small airport a little ways from the city. We just helped ourselves to a plane. My brother knew enough about flying to get us this far. We didn't have time to fill the tanks, and we ran out of fuel just outside the village. He brought her down on a dirt road a couple of miles from here. We knew a train would have to stop here, so we decided to wait for one to show up, hoping it would be friendly. On the way over here, we talked to a farmer who says the coal stop is manned by some soldiers loyal to the dictator."

Kim replied, "Okay, go back to the boxcar. Jake, Ingrid, and Sue are there."

Quint jumped down to the track bed and waved at the twins to follow him, yelling up to Kim, "We can use a couple more guns if we run into trouble."

The fireman climbed back up to the engine, telling the engineer the tank was full, and they were ready to go. Looking back at the tracks and not seeing anyone, the engineer pushed the throttle to the max. The old steam engine spun its massive drive wheels and began the slow assent out of the deep valley.

The fireman shoveled the coal as fast as he could to keep the steam boilers putting out enough steam to keep moving up the steep grade.

Kim asked the engineer, "Are we going to go any slower than we are now?"

"No, this is the worst part until we get to the coal stop."

That didn't make Kim feel any better. If the train went any slower they'd be stopped, a prime target for an ambush.

Just as Kim thought the train was going to stop, the engineer said, "We'll start picking up speed in another hundred yards."

The first and second shots hit the fireman in the shoulder and leg. He dropped his shovel as he fell to the deck.

The next volley of bullets hit the engine stack, ricocheting into the engine compartment.

That volley was followed by another, stitching the boxcar from front to rear. Then the shooting stopped. As they knelt down to help the wounded fireman, Kim yelled at the engineer, "What the hell was that all about?"

The train began picking up enough speed to outrun anyone on foot. It would be nearing its maximum in short order.

"The bullets were sent to us by bandits, not soldiers. They hang out here, and when we have a long train, they pick a couple of cars to rob. We don't resist because the goods aren't worth dying for, and they aren't greedy. That little display was to show us they were still there and dangerous. I think it was an accident they hit the fireman. If we have any trouble, it will be at the coal station."

Jake didn't have time to slide the doors shut on the boxcar before the shooting ceased.

Sue had the handheld radio and called Kim. "What the hell?"

Using Quint's radio, Kim responded, "Bandits, according to the engineer. Not a problem—that will come at the coal station, if at all. After that, the next trouble will be at the border. The coal supply depot is a couple of hours away. How are the twins doing?"

"They seem a little strange. I can't put my finger on it, but there's something going on with them."

"Tell Quint and Jake about the bad vibes and keep an eye on them."

"Ten-four. See you at the coal stop."

Sue laid the radio down and motioned for Quint to join her.

"Have you sensed anything odd about the twins?" she asked in a low voice.

Quint looked over at the twins sitting by the open door of the boxcar and said, "I haven't given it any thought. Do you have some vibes about them?"

"Yes. I don't know what it is, but it's there."

"Okay, I'll keep an eye on them and bring Jake and Ingrid in on this. Now that I think about it, showing up at the water stop was a little too convenient."

Sue added, "Who would have even known we were on the train after all the confusion at the railyard? And then have the resources and time to put something together to stop us?"

Quint winked at Sue, gave her a hug that was more than a friendly gesture, and remarked, "There are only two people besides Hat and No Hat that would know about the timing of the train and who was on it."

"So did the fact that I have a wounded shoulder enter your empty head when you gave me that overly friendly embrace? But although it did hurt, it felt good at the same time, and I'm looking forward to a quick recovery once we get out of this mess, which will be your signal for another session to put out the fire. Cocktails, dinner, dancing, another cocktail, and then to the firehouse.

"Are you referring to the engineer and the fireman as those two people?"

"Yes. You got it. I'll go up to the engine and get with Kim before we reach the coal storage stop. One of them must have a radio or cell phone we don't know about—if they are the guilty party."

"Damn if we don't have a lot of holes in such a small group," replied Sue.

Quint climbed back up the engine again and found Kim stoking the fire. He didn't look up; he was too busy being a pinch hitter for the wounded fireman. The hotter the fire, the more steam from the boilers to keep the train at maximum speed.

The engineer yelled out to Kim over the noise of the engine, "You'll need to tell your friend to spell you with the shoveling."

As Quint walked up, Kim threw him the shovel. "Here you go, mate, it's your turn." Quint caught the shovel and told Kim to tell the engineer to put the train on auto pilot for a few minutes and feed the fire. "We need to talk, Kim, like now!"

Kim relayed the message to the engineer, who locked the throttle in max, grabbed the shovel, and went to work.

Quint explained what he and Sue had decided, and suggested they look around for a radio and more weapons.

Kim remarked, "If he is a loyalist, I bet the attackers on the train back there were not bandits, but rebels for the cause of freedom, a little late with their attack. Lucky for us. You go ahead and feed the furnace, and I'll check out the engine compartment for a phone."

Quint relieved the engineer, and Kim began a search of the compartment, trying not to be obvious. It didn't take him long to find a handheld radio sitting next to a cell phone stowed away under a bunch of rags. The engineer was watching Kim, and began to squirm at the throttle.

Kim picked up the radio, walked over to the engineer, and asked, "What do you use this for?"

He answered, "It's used to call the railyard, the coal stop, and the water storage facilities."

"And the cell phone?"

"I don't use that. It belongs to the fireman."

The fireman was sitting with his back to the rear of the engine compartment, and when Kim turned around to confront him about the cell phone, he pulled a gun and shot Kim in the leg.

Quint saw the fireman pull the gun, but he was too late to stop the shot. His shovel hit the fireman in the head as he pulled the trigger for a second try. The bullet found its way to the engineer, striking him in the right arm.

Quint used his .45 to finish off the wounded fireman with a round to the chest. He pulled the body over to the open doorway and threw the stiff out for roadkill.

Kim hobbled over to the engineer and relieved him of the throttle. He'd learned enough by observing the engineer to keep the train moving.

The engineer fell to the deck, holding his arm and yelling to Kim he didn't know about the gun, repeating that the cell belonged to the dead fireman.

Kim didn't believe him. "I'm going to kill you if there's an ambush at the coal storage stop. You'll be the first one to die."

The engineer yelled for mercy, and at the same time pulled a knife with his good arm and tried to stab Kim. Quint turned in time to put a bullet in the engineer's neck, knocking him backwards. He fell into the furnace, burning up quicker than in a crematorium.

Kim found the engineer's seat and rested his wounded leg as he kept the throttle locked in full ahead.

Quint tied his belt around Kim's leg and remarked, "Well, Jake and I are the only fuckers here without a bullet hole. You guys are becoming a drag, bleeding all over everything. Jesus, you're supposed to duck when someone is shooting at you. Good thing he was a lousy shot."

"Quint, just fix the tourniquet, okay?"

"Damn, Kim, this is no time to lose your sense of humor."

Quint put Kim's leg on a tool chest and radioed for Sue to tell Jake to come up to the engine.

Sue responded, "Do you think we should go ahead and do something with the twins?"

"We've had quite a time up here. I'll explain later. You and Ingrid keep a gun ready in case they become a problem. Don't hesitate to shoot."

Jake took over the throttle duties as Quint helped Kim sit on a small stool by the coal bin and then started feeding the furnace to keep the boilers hot and the steam coming. The coal layover wasn't far away according to the last sign Kim had seen, and Quint suggested, "I think we should stop aways from the coal storage facility and do a recon."

Jake pulled the throttle back, and with the steep incline easily brought the train to a stop. He helped Quint take Kim down to the boxcar.

While Sue was keeping an eye on the twins, Ingrid inspected Kim's wound. She thought the bullet was lodged in the back of the thigh and could easily be removed. They rolled him over, and Ingrid performed a quick surgery. The bullet nearly fell from the leg. After stopping the bleeding, she took the first aid kit and bandaged the wound.

Kim smiled stoically during the procedure, and when it was over, he asked, "Well, doc, will I live, and can I keep the bullet?"

Ingrid gave Kim a slight grin. "Well, Kim, I've done my best. If you don't get an infection, yes, you'll live. And here's the bullet."

Quint patted Kim on the shoulder and motioned for Jake to follow him. "It's time for our recon. You guys keep an eye on Hat and No Hat. One false move earns them a bullet."

They exited the boxcar, heading up the track to the crest of the steep incline to take a look at the coal storage facility.

"Holy cow!" Jake exclaimed. "You see what I see? Damn, there must be a whole fucking battalion of soldiers down there."

The area was crawling with uniformed soldiers from the dictator's army. They'd placed an old truck and railroad ties across the track a couple of hundred yards past the coal tower.

Quint frowned and let out a long breath. "Murphy just rained on our parade. How the hell are we going to get past that?"

Jake said glumly, "I've tried to think of a quote from the winner of a battle that seemed to be doomed for defeat from the beginning. I can't think of any that would fit this situation, except the one by a Marine in Korea who said something like; 'We're surrounded— the sons of bitches can't get away now,' or something like that. Man we're between a rock and a hard place. We need some help from a higher authority."

Quint asked, "Do you think we can run the train through that flimsy junk on the tracks? I don't think it was made to stop the engine, but to slow us down."

"Well, even if we run the blockade, we need a load of coal to keep the damn train running. Since we killed the engineer, we don't know how far the train will go with the remaining coal."

As they were bouncing ideas off each other, the sound of gunfire erupted from the coal storage facility.

Quint used the binoculars to see where the gunfire was coming from and said, "Higher authority has just arrived. The rebels, in a mass, have attacked the loyalist soldiers of the dictator. Jesus, there are hundreds of them. How did they come to be here?"

"Who gives a shit?" retorted Jake. "They came right on cue to save our asses. Maybe Sunny wanted to take control of the railroad tracks to keep the army from coming up from the south. Thinking of that, what do we do if we actually get the opportunity to replenish our coal supply, head down the track, and then run into a train coming up from the other direction? We might want to take note of any sidings where we could get off the main rails."

They had a ringside seat for the battle going on below.

Quint said, "Damn good thing we stopped to take a peek, or we'd be in some deep shit right now."

The dictator's soldiers were falling back a little at a time to the coal storage area, where there were limited fortifications, as the rebels pushed forward.

The sun was on the verge of dipping behind the mountains to the south, and the fight would be in the dark shortly. It would give the rebels the advantage, because the soldiers were surrounded. Flares would soon start lighting up the area, giving the rebels a target that had nowhere to go.

Jake whispered to Quint, "How can we get in contact with the rebel leaders?"

"What the hell are you whispering for? We are at least half a mile from the conflict."

"Hell, I don't know. Just seemed natural. Force of habit from previous clandestine ops. What difference does it make?"

"If Kim was able, he could sneak down there and find someone to help us get on down the track. So I guess we'll have to figure another way to get the fuck out of here."

As the sun disappeared, the first flare burst over the trapped soldiers, followed by mortar and machine gun fire. Tracers lit up the night sky.

Quint suggested, "I'll go back down to the train and see how they are doing. You stay up here and keep an eye on things. If the fight is over before dawn, we might have Kim sit in the engine as we pull into the storage area. I don't think they would destroy the train, because it would benefit them to have the transportation. Time will tell. I'll be back in a few."

Quint disappeared into the night, as the light show below made eerie shadows across the valley, turning night into day, followed by total darkness until the next flare or tracer found its way between the two battling groups.

When Quint approached the boxcar, Kim yelled, "Halt out there," in his native tongue and in English.

Quint yelled back, "Yankee Doodle Dandy."

Kim said, "Okay, Quint, I see you now. We have a problem here. The twins disappeared about an hour ago. They ganged up on Sue and slipped out the open door. I heard the noise but couldn't get a shot off. Ingrid did, but missed. None of us could chase them. They heard the battle going on over the hill, and wanted to help or desert, not sure which."

"Is Sue okay?"

"Yes, just a knot on her head."

Quint jumped up into the boxcar, walked over to Sue, and said, "Well, there you go again. Damn if you don't stay in trouble. Are you okay?"

"Hell yes, I'm okay, no thanks to your running off all the time avoiding the action." She smiled and added, "Are we in some serious shit here or what?"

Quint explained what was happening. If the good guys won as expected, they'd fire up the engine and head down the hill. But for now he should get back and inform Jake the twins were on the loose. He didn't want Jake to be surprised by an ambush.

"I'll be back when the battle has been decided. Keep an eye out, I don't want to come back here to find any more problems."

When Quint was nearly up to the crest where Jake should be watching the valley, he heard muffled gunshots and the shout of someone hit.

"Jake, Jake!" he yelled as he stumbled over the rocks and brush in his hurry. When he came up to their observation spot, Jake was sitting aways below with a knife in his shoulder and the twins lying at his feet.

"What the hell, Jake? Jesus. I hurried to warn you the twins had slipped away from the boxcar. What happened?"

"Well, first things first. How about pulling the knife out of my shoulder? Then, if I don't bleed to death, I'll tell you why I'm wounded and these two lowlife assholes are fucking dead. You'll have to excuse my

French. I'm a little tired and probably in shock, aside from being totally pissed that I let them get this close to me. I'm better than that."

Quint gently pulled the knife out of Jake's shoulder and pressed the wound with his handkerchief. Then he took the shirt and belt off No Hat to cover the wound and bind it.

"How do you feel now?"

"Okay. You must feel lucky, being the only one without a knife or a bullet in you. Would you mind sharing your secret, so we can all avoid such things in the future? Is it black magic, angels, expertise, or maybe just dumbass luck?"

"Can the shit, Jake. Tell me how the battle is going and how you managed to kill these two."

"Relax, Quint! I'll get to it. I'm the one full of holes here."

"Jake!"

"Okay, okay! If you'll slip up the hill a little you can see the fighting has tapered off considerably. I think the bad guys are about to be overrun.

"Now for these two. I was sitting there minding my own business, watching the battle below, and thinking about history. Did you know that during the Civil War, people used to come out to the battlefield in their buggies, dressed in their Sunday best, to watch the conflict?

"Anyway, I smelled the enemy. It was unmistakable. Their diet gave them away. I slipped down to where I am now, hoping they hadn't seen me. I had no idea who was out there, I just knew it couldn't be good. After a few minutes I heard breathing, and the smell of fear was in the air. I knew that whoever it was, he was so scared, so full of adrenalin, he was about to pee his pants.

"A figure came over the crest of the hill while I was looking down the back side, not expecting someone from the other direction. The knife hit me as I put my .45 in his armpit and pulled the trigger. He fell on me, which was a good thing, for the second attacker stuck his knife in the back of his buddy and not me.

"It was pitch black, and he thought he'd stabbed me. Big mistake on his part. As he rolled what he thought was my dead body off his partner, I shoved the .45 into his gut and fired one round. It didn't kill him right away, so I took the knife out of the body lying next to me and cut his throat. He didn't make any noise after that. I was hoping there weren't any more, because I was running out of strength. When you showed up, I thought it was lights out for me.

"That's how it went down for me. I didn't know these two unwashed, foul-smelling shitbirds were Hat and No Hat. Serves them right, lowlife bastards."

Quint asked, "How do you feel? I need to crawl up to the crest and take another look at the goings on. If it looks like there's a lull in the fighting because the good guys have won, we'll head back to the train and see about getting down to the coal stop."

Jake motioned for Quint to go and said, "I'll start back down to the train; no use in me just sitting here. See you back at the boxcar." He turned and made his way down the hill.

Quint crawled up to the crest. Looking down at the coal storage facility, he could see lights coming on along the coal bin and administrative building. The good guys were rounding up the men in uniform and pushing them into an outbuilding. The number of soldiers was small; they had either fought to the death, or the rebels didn't want any prisoners to take care of.

He turned and headed back to the train. As he approached the train, he could see shadows in the darkness around the train. He knew that wouldn't be any of the wounded team. He ducked behind a formation of rocks not far from the track, thinking it would be best to see who was in charge.

After observing the car for an hour, he saw Jake jump down to the track bed and walk towards the trail they'd used to find the crest. When he was near enough to hear a whisper Quint said to him, "What the fuck's going on?"

"I was looking for you. Thought you might not come in if you saw all the activity around the train. Why the hell are you whispering?"

"Not funny, Jake."

"The good guys won the battle and control the coal. We've been waiting for you to come back. The people here were sent by Sunny to take the train south and keep the loyalists from using the track to bring reinforcements north. Sunny told them if they ran into us to take us to the border and do whatever it took to see us to safety. Soon as we board, we'll head down, refuel the coal, and be on our way. It's not more than the rest of tonight and part of tomorrow to the border, but they think it would be best to wait until dark tomorrow to attempt a border crossing."

Relieved, Quint said, "Let's go, I can't wait to find the border and get the hell out of this snake pit. How's the knife wound?'"

"It feels okay I guess; I don't have anything to compare it to."

Approaching the engine, it was obvious someone knew a little about steam engines. The stack was smoking, and there was steam coming from all the leaks in the piping system.

Two men came out to greet them. Jake introduced Quint to the leader of the rebels, who spoke perfect English.

"Hello, Quint. Nice to meet you. I'm from Seattle. I hear you're from up in Blaine. Nice to have a friendly face among this lot. Sunny sends his regards. It's time to get moving—we want to be near the border before dark tomorrow."

They all turned and boarded the train.

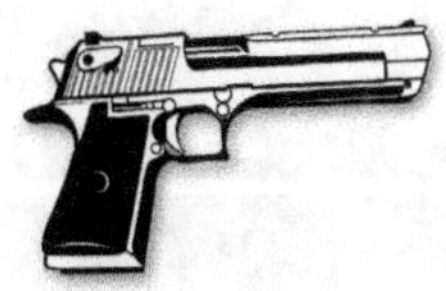

Chapter Thirteen

The Border

The steam engine began to spin its big wheels once again, groaning to climb the steep incline, building up speed as it peaked the crest. The walking wounded were in the boxcar, accompanied by a few of the rebels for defensive purposes.

Quint looked around at the bandage-clad group and remarked, "I was with a team once in an outnumbered firefight, and when it was over, we looked better than you guys. If we have a problem crossing the border, I have my doubts that we will be of any use on our own behalf. It might benefit us to lie low somewhere for a couple of weeks and heal up. But as you know that's impossible, so we need to come up with some good planning to cover our asses. We can't ask our benefactors to put their lives on the line for our dash across the border. They have their own problems and need all the bodies and firepower they can muster for their struggle.

"I talked to their leader, and he says the tracks still run across the border into the south. There is fencing set up like the one that was between East and West Germany in days of old. The two fences are about forty yards apart. There is a triangle set of old railroad rails welded to the track on the north side of the border. He thinks we can run through that and keep going if we get up enough steam to drive the engine full throttle.

"I told their leader we'd take over the train before we get to the border and give it a go. He protested a bit, but finally agreed he needed his men for the coming battles and we should be okay if we get our speed up."

Sue remarked, "Their leader may have had second thoughts about his men reaching the south and not coming back. They would be free and maybe not as committed as he would like."

"That may be the case. I don't know. We need to decide now the course we need to take. We are going to have to breach a secure, fortified and manned border without an army with us."

Jake stood up, wincing from the knife wound. "What's the fucking problem? We fire up the furnace as hot as it will get; the steam will push those big-ass wheels at a terrific speed. We start shooting every-thing we have at the border guards and plow through the barricade. They'll be so surprised it'll be a piece of cake."

"You know, Jake, leave it to you to bring everything down to the basics. He's right of course. We don't have many options. Walking across is not possible, and we don't have a plane or ship.

"Sue, Ingrid, any ideas?"

They both shrugged their shoulders and shook their heads.

The train was barreling down the track, in a hurry to end its journey as the round-eyed intruders licked their wounds and looked forward to returning to the civilized world.

Quint was asked to climb up to the engine to meet with the rebel leader on their plans for the border crossing.

"Quint, this afternoon we'll be nearing the place where we'll stop the train and my troops will get off. You'll be on your own from that point on. What are your plans? Our forces will be attacking the loyalists right behind you."

Quint was slow to answer, not sure he wanted to take the action they'd decided on.

"My friend, we will be driving the train through the fences and barrier. Maybe we can create some confusion to assist you in your attack. Hopefully, the engine plows through the rails welded to the track, and the bad guys on the other side don't kill us."

"Okay, Quint. When this is all over I'll look you up at the gun shop in Blaine. I had to come here to help my people find the freedom that I have enjoyed. Good luck."

The train picked up more speed as a downgrade made the engine's job easier. Quint climbed back down to the boxcar to let everyone know the charge of the boxcar brigade would begin later in the afternoon.

"When the train stops, Jake and I will man the engine. Kim, you and Ingrid be ready to shoot everything you've got out the open doors. Sue, you feed them ammo and anything else they need. Try to keep your heads down when they start shooting back. When the border guards see the train has no intention of stopping, they'll throw everything they have at us. The rebels will attack right behind us; maybe they'll take some of the heat off, but don't plan on it. If the engine doesn't smash through the welded old rails, we'll be in deep shit."

Quint hadn't gotten the last words out before whoever was manning the engine slammed the throttle into reverse, throwing everyone forward. They rolled into the walls, trying not to yell out in pain.

Quint picked himself up and looked to see if the others had additional injuries. Everyone gave the thumbs-up sign. He looked out the open door of the boxcar to see what the hell had prompted the sudden slowdown. He could see up ahead that another train had pulled onto the track siding and yelled to the others, "Hit the deck, we're about to get a volley of gunfire!"

His warning was none too soon. As they hit the deck, a full-scale barrage hit the train. The engineer had tried to stop before coming abreast of the track siding, but was too late.

The train was going too slow and an easy target, so the engineer pushed the throttle to the max. But trains aren't dragsters; it takes time to get them up to speed.

The rebels were firing back with everything they had, which slowed down the incoming. The walking wounded gathered themselves to fire back as well while the train slowly passed the siding.

Quint didn't see them jump off the train, but most of the rebels jumped before they reached the siding, and were now attacking the other train from the ground.

The train was finally gaining some speed when the engineer slammed on the brakes, sending everyone forward once more. When he finally got the engine stopped, the bullets were pinging off the boxcar. He put the train in reverse and began to back up to join the ground troops in the battle with the other train.

The loyalist train had one engine, five boxcars, two flat cars and a caboose. The soldiers on it were outgunned by the rebels, and the battle didn't last long.

Quint had jumped down when their train stopped and ran into the battle, trying to save the engineer on the dictator's train. They could use him when they bashed their way across the border.

He was too late; the engineer and fireman were dead, along with the signalman. The rebel leader said, "Now I have enough room for all my troops. I'll take the captured train back up the tracks and pick up the rest of my people. If you'll wait here, maybe we can help you with the run on the border. We're going to have plenty of firepower."

Quint agreed to stay until they returned.

The one-car train pulled ahead again to allow the captured train to pull onto the tracks behind them.

The cell phone rang for the first time in a couple of days. It startled Quint as he wondered who the hell could be calling. "Quint here."

"My friend and leader of the rebels who helped you told me what was going on with the trains. There's no need to wait for him. All but two of the dictator's air force defected to the south. The two that didn't blew up his train. We don't know where the fighters have gone, so I suggest you get your train moving with a full head of steam as you hit the border. Need to go."

Quint could sense the sadness in Sunny's voice and the determination to continue the battle for his people's freedom.

"Jake, Kim, let's get up to the engine. Some air force jets loyal to the dictator are on the loose. We need to get moving; the other train won't be joining us."

Jake asked, "Do we draw straws to see who's going to be the driver? I can use my left arm on the throttle. We don't need to worry about applying the brakes, since we're going to plow through the border fortifications.

"Actually since only one of us is whole, it is logical to assume Quint would be the one to shovel the coal into the furnace. So I guess we don't need to draw straws."

Quint looked at Jake with raised eyebrows and confusion. "What the hell was all that convoluted bullshit you just shared?"

Jake responded, "Bottom line, my friend: you're the fireman. Now grab a shovel and feed the furnace. I'll cover the throttle part, and Kim will shoot the enemy."

Quint and Kim grinned and took their respective positions.

Kim, using the handheld, called down to Sue and Ingrid, "Keep an eye out for two jet fighters that may be heading our way."

Jake said, "Wait, we have to switch the tracks."

Quint sighed, "Damn, a one-man train crew. Hold on, I'll go."

While Quint was switching the tracks back to the main line, he looked up to see a couple of dots coming from the north, and yelled to the others, "Incoming aircraft. Get moving, Jake."

Jake shoved the throttle to full ahead, and the short train began to chug along the main line.

Quint jumped onto the engine when the first jet unloaded on the siding, missing them by a hundred yards.

The second jet came in low, continued on past, and crashed into the mountain ahead of them.

They could see the pilot had ejected and was floating down near the crest of the slight grade.

Quint looked around and didn't see the first jet anywhere. Then he heard another explosion.

"I bet those jets ran out of fuel." He went on to say, "If the dictator was half smart he wouldn't have left any aircraft on the tarmac with enough fuel to fly very far. These guys should have checked their gauges."

Jake kept the throttle on full ahead and asked, "Do we stop for the downed pilot?"

Quint kept the shovel moving as he responded, "We don't need any distractions. Keep her rolling."

The train was running at maximum speed, with the last ten miles a downhill grade, increasing their speed. It was becoming dangerous at such high speeds, because the track bed was old and not well maintained.

Quint had slowed down feeding the furnace. "Jake, we might have reached capacity here. This old steam engine may come apart if we go any faster."

"What the hell, Quint, we're gonna die when we hit the fortified border anyway. We might as well make it spectacular."

Kim shouted over the noise of the rumbling engine, "Sue and Ingrid want to know if they should say their prayers."

Jake shouted back. "The border is in sight, we'll know soon enough. Tell them to prepare for impact."

The ancient engine was gasping its last as the boiler and furnace began to come apart, spewing water, coal, and steam out both sides of the track hitting the border guards with hot steam and boiling water. Their weapons dropped as they fled from the out-of-control train.

They plowed through the first fence, dragging hundreds of feet of it along with them. The old rails welded at angles on the track didn't stop their progress south. They sliced through neatly, sending them flying to either side of the engine. The second fence was the last obstacle before the train crossed over the border, but the impact with the rails caused the engine to start coming apart, and the big drive wheels collapsed, bringing the train to a sudden stop a good thirty yards short of the border fence. Jake yelled out, "The gauge on the boiler is pegged in the red, it's going to blow! We better get the fuck out of here!"

Quint helped Kim down to the railroad bed. It was easy because the engine was sitting on the tracks with the huge wheels flat on the ground."

Jake jumped down, and they ran back to the boxcar to get Sue and Ingrid.

As they reached the boxcar, gunfire erupted from both sides of the border, the north trying to kill them and the south trying to suppress the fire from the north.

Sue and Ingrid jumped out of the car, putting it between them and the north's barrage.

Looking across the open space they could see a huge crowd gathering to cheer them on to freedom, waving and shouting encouragement for them to reach the border.

Sue remarked, "Well, Quint, let's hear some inspiring shit about how we can dodge the bullets and slip under the fence to freedom."

Quint grinned. Sue, what does your woman's intuition tell you?"

"It tells me you better come up with something soon, since you're the only one here who can run faster than a turtle."

Jake butted in, "How about canning all the tit-for-tat crap, and put your minds to something more important than your visions of cocktails and dinner. This is serious shit here."

Kim said, "Not a problem. We hold out until dark and crawl the rest of the way. If they don't drop some heavy stuff on us, we can wait it out. When the spotlights come on, we shoot them out, or our friends on the south side will. I've seen people in situations similar to this before. Darkness will be our friend in this case."

Ingrid, who had more experience with border crossings than anyone else, agreed with Kim. "Tonight we'll be able to reach the fence. Except for one small problem. It's probably mined."

Quint let out a long sigh. "Shit, I never thought of that."

Jake spoke up again. "I used to be in the combat engineers. I'll crawl out there with the knife the twins tried to kill me with, and I'll probe for and disable any mines, making a path for us to follow. Piece of cake."

Sue shot back, "You're going to do this in the dark? And if you blow yourself up, what then?"

"Not a problem, Sue. Have a little faith. I'm not ready to die in this fucked-up communist country. I wanna live to see the country returned to its people. As I said, piece of cake."

The bullets were still bouncing off the boxcar as the sun disappeared into the ocean, leaving the huge lighting system shining on the border from the north side.

Quint and Kim started shooting out the spotlights, and then the north began shutting them off and on to confuse the issue. Each time they came on Quint and Kim managed to put out a couple more.

Jake began crawling and probing for the mines when the lights were dark, and freezing when they came on. He'd not gone ten feet before he discovered the first mine.

Ingrid was behind him, followed by Sue. Quint and Kim stayed behind giving them covering fire, shooting at the muzzle flashes in the north.

It didn't take Jake long to dismantle the first mine and move on.

The snipers from the north were nearly zeroed in on their positions, so Quint and Kim kept moving, drawing the fire away from their crawling teammates.

The shooters from the south ceased, leaving only the flashes from the north's guns. Quint thought, *I bet the fucking diplomatic corps has gotten involved and told the south to cut the firing to keep from creating a full-scale international incident. Dumbasses. There is a frigging civil war in progress, and they're worried about a couple of people fighting their way across a border that may not be there in a couple of months, if the good guys win.*

"Kim, you make your way over to the trail Jake is leaving. I'll hang out a little longer, taking pot shots to keep them busy."

"Okay, you take care, and don't drag your feet following us."

Kim disappeared into the dark, finding his way around the boxcar to follow Ingrid's tracks.

Jake lost count of the mines he had dismantled and was twenty feet from the fence and freedom when he made a small mistake. Somehow he hadn't released the pressure release piston, and he had to hold it down with his finger. If he released the piston, the mine would explode, taking Sue and Ingrid with him.

He turned his head and quietly said to Sue, "Sue, I need you to crawl over me and on to the fence. I believe this is the last mine between us and the fence. Tell Ingrid to follow you, no questions asked."

"Jesus, Jake, what the hell is going on?"

"I've encountered a small problem. Now get going."

Sue turned to inform Ingrid, who had just been tapped on the leg by Kim, so she passed on the message and followed Sue crawling over Jake.

When Kim got up to Jake he said, "You're the engineer, what can I do to help?"

"Nothing right now. I'll wait for Quint to get here, and we'll figure this out. You go ahead to the fence, and if we need anything, you can bring it back to us."

Kim didn't like the idea of leaving Jake mated with the mine, but there was little to be done, so he crawled up to the fence and joined Sue and Ingrid for their first taste of freedom in weeks.

Many hands reached out to help them, as the others applauded their arrival.

Quint was watching between the on-and-off light shit the north was doing, and he could see there was a problem with Jake and the others. He'd shot nearly all the lights out, but they had night scopes to keep him moving from one spot to another.

When he saw that Jake was the only one left in the open field, he didn't need a PhD to figure he'd fucked up and couldn't let go of the mine. Quint started crawling out to help him. In the meantime Kim and Ingrid started shooting at the snipers and lights, using their own night vision equipment.

When Quint reached Jake, he could tell right away what was up. "Well, is your finger getting tired? I would appreciate it if you'd keep it there a little while longer."

"Quint, may I remind you your life is now in my control? I've always looked at the bright side of things, but right now my sense of humor sucks."

"Okay, my friend; I have an idea how to get your ass out of this mess, and you'll owe me forever. And as I recall this isn't the first time, I've pulled your fat out of the fire."

"Okay, okay. Jesus, Quint, get the fuck on with it."

Quint crawled over Jake like the others and up to the fence, yelling for someone to get him a twenty-five pound square flat weight of some kind.

Kim shouted out what Quint was asking for, and within minutes an old man brought them a flat weight used on weight scales at a local fish market. Kim handed the weight to Quint and said, "Take care, my friend, I'd like to see your smiling face on this side of the border."

"No problem, Kim, we'll do just fine."

When Quint turned to crawl back to Jake, the dawn was minutes away from shining unwanted light over the no-man's-land, giving the north shooters a clear view of their targets.

Jake was beginning to sweat from the continued pressure needed to keep the piston down, and he was very happy to see Quint on his way back.

"Okay Jake, we don't have time for the old saying 'measure twice, cut once.' We have to get it right the first time.

"I'll put the weight on top of your finger. It should weigh enough to keep the piston down when you jerk your finger out. It will move, but I think there is enough play in the piston that it won't release."

"You think! If you're wrong on this one, we'll make the border, but in many pieces."

"I'm confident enough to be here when you pull your finger out. I'll hold the weight to be sure it goes straight down."

As Jake readied himself to pull his finger out, shots rang out, hitting all around them, and getting nearer with each shot.

Kim yelled out, "Can anyone see where the shots are coming from? Damn, they won't have a chance if the rounds get any closer. If Jake or the mine takes a hit, it's over."

Ingrid shouted for all to hear, "The shooter is in the boxcar."

Before the words had left her lips, Kim and the others who'd joined in the suppressive fire sent a volley at the old car, pelting it with a hundred rounds. The shooting stopped.

Kim encouraged them to continue the onslaught and keep the north shooter hunkered down until Jake and Quint could escape the deadly mine.

"Jake, it's time to pull your finger. I have the weight in position. Don't worry about the incoming rounds. Our problem is way more important than that lame-ass shooter."

"Do you have anything to confess, before I pull my finger? You know, Quint, something on your mind that you need to unload before you see your maker?"

"If I wanted to confess, I would find a chaplain. Jake, get on with it. Jerk your finger out."

Jake slipped his hand out from under the weight, allowing the weight to replace his finger.

Quint took a breath for the first time in minutes as he felt the weight drop and watched Jake roll over, turning his back to the likely explosion.

After a tense pause, Quint turned towards the border and started crawling for all he was worth, followed by Jake, who had to stand and jump over the mine, drawing gunfire from the north. His smile of relief was unmistakable.

The bullets hit all around the duo, and then the shooter got smart and tried to hit the mine, but the weight on top protected it from the bullets.

When they reached the fence and freedom, Jake stood and was giving the finger to the north soldiers just as the mine blew up, knocking him down and sending small pieces of shrapnel into the crowd. A large piece hit Quint in the side.

He yelled out to Jake, "You give those guys the finger, it pisses them off, and they shoot better. Now I've been hit. Why don't you moon them, and see if they shoot even better?"

Jake's shoulder was still hurting but he took Quint up on his idea and mooned the north.

"How's that, you lowlife fuckin' commie bastards!" Jake yelled across no-man's-land.

Sue took Quint by the hand and led him to an aid station that had been put up in case a fullscale battle erupted at the border. "Well, my friend, it looks like we'll be having dinner and cocktails after all," she remarked.

"Not so fast, Sue. Maybe we should heal up before we start close dancing, and the excitement created by the contact opens our wounds."

"Damn, that little chicken-shit scratch you have wouldn't leak enough blood to take a sugar test."

Jake butted in, "We've been summoned by the local authorities. They want to know what the fuck is going on."

"Soon as I get patched up, we'll head over to the American embassy. We'll want their representation on this one," Quint replied.

Chapter Fourteen

The Cabal

After an afternoon with the embassy people, the team managed to book flights to California.

Ingrid contacted the trawler captain and arranged for her funds to be sent to a bank in Idaho. She wanted to live someplace where the weather was nearly like her hometown. The embassy, with some pressure from the Cabal, gave her the opportunity to become an American citizen.

Kim returned to Canada, where he waited for Sunny to keep him posted on what he could do to help continue their quest for freedom.

Jake flew back to Blaine from California and resumed his work at the gun shop.

Quint and Sue stood in the lobby of the Cabal office building waiting for the secretary to announce them to the board of directors.

Sue glanced at Quint standing next to her in a business suit, looking more like a Wall Street broker than a covert field agent working for a company dedicated to helping the world free itself from the evil that most world leaders wouldn't face.

She smiled now that they were out of serious danger and their wounds were healed. The coming evening was evoking memories of past experiences.

Quint looked down at her and smiled, squeezing her hand and whispering, "You are beautiful, sexy, and the fire is burning brightly within. Do you suppose we can find time to fan the flames?"

Just then the secretary entered and interrupted the electricity flowing between them. "The Cabal is ready for you in the board room. Please follow me."

She led them through the huge doors into a well-lit room, where the couple found themselves standing in front of a long table with ten chairs and nine men.

The spokesman for the group addressed them: "We are happy that two of our finest agents, who fight crime and evil wherever they find it, are safe and whole. Although you accomplished your mission, there was considerable collateral damage that we, and I suppose you, didn't intend.

The future of the country is still in doubt, but according to the reports we've received, the good guys may succeed.

"For now, take a month off. Sue, after your vacation, come back to the offices and your chair at the table. Quint, enjoy the time off and be ready for more work."

The lights dimmed, and the men at the table departed.

The secretary returned and escorted Quint and Sue out of the room and down the hall to the elevator. She pushed the down button and said, "See you in a month."

Quint waited until the elevator doors closed before he took Sue into his arms, crushing her with a bear hug.

Sue whispered in his ear, "Let's go put the fire out and keep the coals burning."

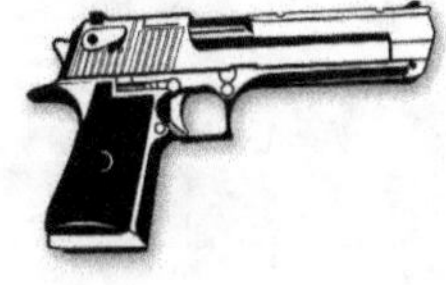

*"Liberty, when it begins to take root,
is a plant of rapid growth."*
George Washington

About the Author

R. Michael Haigwood is a Marine veteran, life member and past Commandant of the Black Mountain Detachment, Marine Corps League. He worked on many construction projects as a member of the International Union of Operating Engineers, Local 12, from which he is retired. He is a longtime resident of Las Vegas, where he lives with his partner, Jean.

www.ingramcontent.com/pod-product-compliance
Lightning Source LLC
Chambersburg PA
CBHW071747190726
48292CB00003B/895